As tender as the night...

Slowly turning her palms up to meet his lips,
Jeremy continued to kiss her hands softly, gently,
as one might kiss a child frightened by some
terrible dream. Still holding her hands in his, he
rose slowly, so that she, too, stood up and found
herself a hairbreadth from him.

Aviva's eyes did not move to his face but simply
considered the intricate pattern of his sweater.
Then his lips began to explore her face, roaming
over her smooth brow, nestling in her scented hair.

"My poor darling," he whispered. "My poor, lovely
woman. Don't be afraid to love again. Love me now."

ABOUT THE AUTHOR

Rebecca Bond holds an M.B.A. in marketing
and has worked as an advertising copywriter,
as well as an advertising account executive.
Her passion is traveling, which she feels
helps her in her writing; she has been all
over the world, including China and Japan.
A native Californian, Rebecca lives in Los
Angeles with her husband, a federal prosecutor.

Books by Rebecca Bond

HARLEQUIN AMERICAN ROMANCE
 92—IN PASSION'S DEFENSE
109—BED AND BOARD

These books may be available at your local bookseller.

Don't miss any of our special offers. Write to us at the
following address for information on our newest releases.

Harlequin Reader Service
P.O. Box 52040, Phoenix, AZ 85072-2040
Canadian address: P.O. Box 2800, Postal Station A,
5170 Yonge St., Willowdale, Ont. M2N 6J3

Bed
and Board
REBECCA BOND

Harlequin Books

TORONTO • NEW YORK • LONDON
AMSTERDAM • PARIS • SYDNEY • HAMBURG
STOCKHOLM • ATHENS • TOKYO • MILAN

Published July 1985

First printing May 1985

ISBN 0-373-16109-3

Chapter One

"Be careful!" Aviva Thompson called as she prowled back and forth over the red brick walk. Her fingers were laced visorlike over her eyes as she guarded them against the bright early spring sun. Unconsciously, she bit into her full lower lip as she watched Tim work high above her. Lowering her hands for a moment, she shivered involuntarily against the morning chill and gazed out toward the ocean. Aviva, smiling to herself, surveyed the low-lying fog, which swirled like the lace of some antique wedding veil blown in the breeze over the bluffs that stood guard at the ocean's door.

The surf was high, but there would be no young swimmers braving the icy waters that morning. The sea was unpredictable and easily became a monster alive with menacing swells and currents that would pound the ever-changing sands each year. The cypress trees, bent and twisted from years in the wild climate, would again surrender to the force of the sea winds and bow like humble supplicants waiting for the benevolent hand of early fall to bid them rise and face a

new, calmer season. Yet each year they would rise,
ever more slowly, destined never to stand straight
again after centuries of Northern California winters.

Aviva sighed. She loved the weather here in Carmel. It was unlike any experienced by the rest of the
country. There was something noble about the small
town nestled like a gallant young soldier behind the
bluffs, daring the threatening elements to destroy the
stronghold. The constant gray fog only lent charm to
the scene, rather than being forbidding. The fog was
heaven's blanket: protecting, shielding and comforting the intensely private people who inhabited the tiny
coastal hamlet. Even in this modern day and age the
citizens of Carmel by the Sea closely guarded their
privacy and the old ways.

There were no street numbers on the little cottages,
no lights or sidewalks on the residential streets. Only
trees and wildflowers adorned the wide, quiet avenues
where the inhabitants lived. The town of Carmel
hadn't even painted white lines on the asphalt streets.

But no matter how hard the townspeople fought to
keep civilization away, they could not hide the natural
beauty of the place forever. Artisans who had origi-
nally retreated to Carmel for privacy had turned from
the pursuit of pure creation to owning shops that
hawked their wares to the ever-increasing number of
tourists that arrived each year. Downtown Carmel had
become like any other tourist area in California: over-
crowded and oversold. But somehow the quiet personality of the town lingered on, jealously maintained
by those who lived there year-round.

Yes, Aviva thought to herself, hands digging into

the back pockets of her old jeans, *nothing can ever really change Carmel.*

"Mommy, come quick!" Her daughter's high-pitched shriek from inside the house brought Aviva out of her reverie. "Mommy, a rainbow!"

Aviva slowed her pace, realizing that Jenny's scream was not one of alarm. Entering the old house through the heavy carved oak door, she saw her daughter staring up at the third-story window where Tim stood perched precariously on the window molding.

"Mommy, it's so pretty." Her voice was breathless with wonderment.

Gathering Jenny into her arms Aviva nuzzled her face into the soft, long hair. "Yes, we'll always have our own rainbow right in this house."

"Hey, did everybody forget me?" Tim's question floated down from high above them, and they turned to look at his smiling face.

"Of course not." Aviva set her daughter down carefully on the inlaid wood floor. "How can I ever thank you? It's beautiful."

The words seemed somehow incomplete as Aviva looked up at the large stained-glass window Tim had just finished installing. The early-morning light shone down through the fleur-de-lis pattern, splashing a soft red, blue, green and gold rainbow over the octagon entry and the many-layered stairwell above it.

Suddenly Aviva laughed. The giant prism made Tim look like a tattooed man whose colors were running together in the rain.

"Listen, lady," Tim said with a smile as he jumped

down from the sill to greet Jenny, who had run up the three flights of stairs to meet him, "that's six months of hard work you're laughing at. Not only that, but no one ever laughs at a masterpiece by Timothy Greenly, especially when it's free."

With Jenny hanging on his legs, he made his way to the oak railing and leaned over.

"You do know that it was a labor of love, don't you?" he continued, his voice gently serious.

A shadow passed over Aviva's face as she looked up. She hated it when he attempted to become more a part of her life than he should be. The chemistry just wasn't right between them. Aviva was so practical and Tim so...artistic. She didn't want someone to adore her, just someone to challenge her both physically and mentally. Tim just couldn't seem to understand that.

"You are a true friend, sir," she answered lightly, emphasizing the word "friend" in the hope of steering the conversation to a safer topic as her mind raced on.

Tim seemed so young to her and, indeed, she was three years his senior. And at twenty-nine Aviva was more mature than most men or women her age. The past six years had forced her to face the hard realities of life. It wasn't only the untimely death of her husband. Sam had been older, of course, but still, a man as vigorous as he was should not have died at forty-five, especially in the arms of another woman.

Sam the adventurer had been hers for a while, and their marriage had been one exciting moment after another that first year. Aviva had loved it, or thought she did. But when Jenny was born that second year,

Aviva wanted a quieter life. And Sam, dear Sam, the wonder of the commercial production world, had truly tried to accommodate her wish, but it just wasn't in him. He needed the constant stimulus of the new faces and exotic worlds his work offered him. Surrounded by beautiful models, shooting on location, he couldn't help but be impressed by the glamour, especially when he was the center of it.

When he started turning to other women, Aviva had been hurt, distraught that he couldn't understand her needs, that he couldn't grow up and face the responsibilities and joys of family life. But she couldn't leave him. She did love him for all of his faults, just as she had loved her father, whom she had never known. A man, her mother said, very much like Sam. But a man who couldn't stay put for long. The very traits that pained Aviva the wife and mother still thrilled Aviva the woman.

For the first time in her life, though, she had had a man to take care of her. Sam had physically stayed with her and she had everything a woman could want: beautiful clothes, a lovely home in the Hollywood Hills, a child that rivaled a Botticelli angel and a man who truly wanted to care for her in his own way, a man who was handsome and witty and virile. How could she have left all that?

But it was during the funeral, as she stood with Jenny, that she finally realized she should have left Sam and Southern California years ago. Los Angeles was not her world; it was his. He was the sun god, beautiful and full of life, perfectly suited to the constant sunshine that beat down on the sprawling city. It was unnatural, all that sunshine, she had found herself irreverently thinking that day. It made the people of Los Angeles run like mechanical dolls. Run for the sun, the fun, see and be seen, look into all the corners and share everyone's life. Hurry, hurry, because a place that has sunshine all the time eventually will find itself in the dark. And how afraid they were of the dark. How afraid Sam must be, now that he didn't have the sunshine anymore.

"How can I teach Jenny about Christmas?" Aviva had once asked her husband.

"So, what's to teach, babe? Christmas is the time for indulging. Here it's Christmas all year round."

"I mean about the feeling that comes with a brisk, cold day, or seeing carolers wrapped up in warm coats expecting a cup of cocoa for their songs. Here everything is so...so mechanized. If you see something in a store window you can have it. Where's the *feeling*?" Her green eyes had pleaded with him to give her the answer she wanted to a question that encompassed so much more than Christmas.

Sam had come to her and held her close, unable to answer. Wrapping his arms about her he kissed her dark hair. It was his way of telling her that he understood but couldn't share her concern for traditions of the past.

Sam could never think the way she did. They were night and day, as natural for each other as the sun and the moon, and it had seemed that neither could exist without the other. And so they had lived together, accepted each other and loved desperately, and ever more infrequently, until the day he left her.

Aviva carried on with her life, vowing that she would never again trust her future to anyone who couldn't share her ways, love her for what she was. She alone would care for Jenny, instilling in her all the wonderful values that those Southern Californians seemed to have packed away for a rainy day, a day that would never come for most of them. She knew, more than likely, that she would be alone for a long, long time.

In three weeks she had disposed of all their property. The house in the hills had brought $300,000, the production company another large sum. The Mercedes was gone, but Aviva kept the convertible Volkswagen knowing it was more practical. She sold her jewelry and the furniture, and packed the car.

There had only been a few people to say good-bye to. Everyone else was really a friend of Sam's and much too busy at the tennis court or hairdresser to wonder where Aviva Thompson was going. But Aviva knew what was ahead of her. She was going to find a home. With Jenny surrounded by pots and pans, Aviva had headed north, praying that she would find the fairy-tale place she had longed for. Six hours later she had.

The huge house was surrounded by cypress trees. A widow's walk peeked out of the north tower; a wide veranda encircled the entire structure, breaking only where one room extended from the main body of the house onto the plateau above the ocean.

The room was fascinating. It had five sides but no walls—only large windows looking out to sea, sentinels watching for the approach of a long-lost ship. The house stood alone, the wild grass and berry bushes creating a crazy-quilt garden as far as the eye could see.

"Look, Jenny," she had whispered, slipping the car into first gear so she could slowly approach, "it's our new home."

Jenny had clapped her hands, delighted without knowing why. Together, they had wandered around the veranda, peeking into windows crusted with dirt, waving away dust from years of neglect. Aviva tried every door but none would open. Then, grabbing Jenny's hand, she ran with the child to the edge of the bluff to look at the giant rambling structure, and Aviva thought her heart would burst with immediate love for the house.

The sun was settling as the two reluctantly returned to the car and drove on. Aviva was determined to have the house, and Jenny was determined to sleep. Aviva did not have to look far to find the old lawyer who had all but forgotten his duties as executor of the last owner's will and of Whaler's Retreat, as the house was known. The next morning, after a few inquiries in the small town, Aviva was directed to the attorney's office on the outskirts of town. The ancient little man behind the large desk had been wary but kind.

"You're alone, then, Mrs. Thompson...divorced?" he had queried, his eyes appraising her over his rimless glasses.

"No, widowed," she had answered, watching him soften at the admission.

"Just you and the little one, then, in that big old house, out in the middle of nowhere?"

"Mr. Corbet, I would hardly call three miles from town the middle of nowhere, and in a city such as this I don't think there is anything to be afraid of." Aviva had smiled her most ladylike smile.

Mr. Corbet spent the next thirty minutes extolling the virtues of Carmel and the natural fear of strangers coming into the town; there had been too many the past few seasons.

"I assure you, Mr. Corbet, Jenny and I wish to make this our home."

"How are you going to live?"

"I have rather a tidy sum from the sale of our things in Los Angeles." Corbet scoffed through his nose at the mention of L.A. but Aviva continued. "I'm sure that will hold us nicely, depending, of course, on the price of the house."

The lawyer had pulled an old journal from the right-hand drawer of the desk and had begun leafing through the pages.

"It isn't cheap, Mrs. Thompson, especially when you consider the fix-up costs that go with it. You know that old place hasn't got copper pipes—old plumbing, you know—and the roof needs fixing." He didn't look up, and she wondered if he were trying to discourage her. "The price is fixed at three hundred fifty thousand dollars, but that includes the acreage around it. Figure another hundred to two hundred thousand to get it fixed up proper, and then there's the heating costs and—"

"Well, I was intending to renovate it for business purposes." Aviva hadn't considered the future; she didn't know where she was going with her train of thought, she only knew she had to have that house. If what he was saying was true, she and Jenny wouldn't have a dime in a year.

"What kind of mortgage rates are we looking at, Mr. Corbet?"

"Aren't any. Clara made me swear to get cash for the damned thing," he said, flushing at the light expletive. "'Scuse me. Anyway, that was so she'd be sure a good family would move in. She always thought that if someone had money, they had breeding." The little man surveyed her tight jeans and high-heeled boots as he spoke. Aviva could hardly keep herself from squirming in the straight-backed chair.

"I see. Well, that's no problem." She couldn't let him see the disappointment she was feeling.

"What exactly are you planning on doing with it? I hope it won't be another one of those fancy shops that are springing up all over town."

Aviva's mind raced. She reached up and unbuttoned her jacket, stalling for time. "I'm going to—" She hesitated, then the thought hit her. "I'm going to open a boardinghouse, Mr. Corbet, a bed and board where people can enjoy life the way it used to be lived."

He smiled genuinely for the first time and leaned back in his chair, the creak of the wood reassuring her.

"You know what I mean," she hurried on excitedly, "restore the house to its old grandeur . . . no telephones, televisions . . . a fireplace with a chess set in front of it and books in the library. I always wanted to make people feel comfortable when they were away from home."

"Mighty nice," Mr. Corbet mused, his approval and admiration growing with every word she spoke. "You know, Mrs. Thompson, I could have those papers drawn up in no time. Can you move in the first of the week?"

So it had started. Mr. Corbet, her first friend, had introduced her proudly to the "real" people in Carmel: Joe the plumber, who would give her the best price he possibly could, and Bob, who was the handyman about town. Mrs. Jensen would help her with drapes and curtains and, of course, Tim, who would add the finishing touches with his beautiful Tiffany lamps and leaded glass windows.

She and Jenny had cleaned up the kitchen and one bedroom the day they moved in, and for a year they lived as if they were at a perpetual slumber party. The house was torn up and put back together. While the workmen pounded and sawed, tore down and put back up, cleaned and stripped wood, and refinished floors, Aviva was right there beside them. She learned how to replace the antique moldings so that you couldn't see the repair; she gently stripped away the layers of wax to reveal exquisitely ornate hardwood floors inlaid with mahogany squares and triangles. She hunted for just the right furniture and carefully restored the antiques to their original majesty. As the seasons changed, she befriended the townsfolk, slowly gaining their confidence, becoming one of them.

With each old layer of paint and wallpaper that fell to the floor Aviva stripped away the pain of her previous life in Los Angeles. It was as if she had never really lived it, as if she had been born again: a pioneer woman destined to live life alone, caring for her child, earning her keep in a respectable manner, sheltering her world from any and all intruders.

Now she stood, together with the two people she cared about most in the world—the daughter she loved and the friend she respected. She stood in her house, her boardinghouse, and looked about her.

The brass sconces on the wall were polished to perfection, the Oriental rugs were in place over the gleaming floors, a fire burned like a welcoming beacon in the living room, and a silver bowl filled to overflowing with flowers stood on the long dining-room table.

More importantly, Tim's creation, the huge window, now seemed to offer a blessing to the house and all those in it. It was perfect, except for one thing— Aviva was almost broke. Along with the pride that flooded her heart and soul was the black demon of doubt. How could she ever fill the twelve rooms upstairs year-round?

"All right you two, we're finally finished and tonight we are going to have a celebration." She forced the concern to the back of her mind. This was a day for celebration. She had come this far on her own; she would go the rest of the way.

"Tim, I want you back here at seven dressed in your Sunday best and don't you dare bring a hammer or a saw or even a nail into this place tonight. If it isn't finished by now, it's never going to be."

"Yes, ma'am." Tim came to attention and saluted as if to a drill sargeant. Jenny awkwardly drew her pudgy hand to her forehead, attempting to mimic the tall, bearded man.

"Yes, ma'am," came her high voice.

Aviva bent down, took the rosy face between her hands, and planted a kiss over both eyes.

"Hey." Tim touched her shoulder timidly. "I had something to do with all this, too."

Aviva hesitated for only a moment and then gave Tim her most sincerely platonic kiss on his cheek, then withdrew taking Jenny's hand.

"Now scoot, mister, I have a date with the kitchen," she commanded happily.

It was four when Aviva had finally finished setting the long table. The "new" antique china was perfect. Sprigs of lavender adorned the rim of the plates and a delicate ribbon of gold outlined the fluted coffee cups. The crystal wine, champagne and water glasses were mismatched, but the intricate etching of each complemented the others. For Jenny, Aviva had splurged and bought a silver milk mug dancing with carved figures of ducks and rabbits. Aviva had Jenny's initials engraved on the bottom—something for her to give her baby, if she ever married.

Aviva, unable to resist, popped the oven door open and found the beef Wellington coming along nicely. The pastry was slowly browning to perfection. Heart of palm salad—not easy to come by—was chilling in the refrigerator and all the ingredients were ready for the Grand Marnier soufflé. Surveying her handiwork, she realized that at least one good thing had come out of her time in Los Angeles. That cooking school Sam had insisted she attend to get her out of the house during her pregnancy had been fun, but now it was also proving to be profitable. Whaler's Inn would be known for its food as well as its warm hospitality, thanks to that outrageously expensive course.

Hands on hips, she surveyed the table and mentally checked her list: candles, flowers, brandy, coffee. She hoped Tim would not misunderstand her invitation. Aviva longed for a quiet evening of good food and good company—nothing more.

Sighing contentedly, she turned toward the stairway and climbed the carpeted stairs to the third floor. She had two hours to herself before she had to wake Jenny from her nap to get her ready for the gala evening. Two hours all to herself—and she was going to take advantage of each minute.

"THE DINNER WAS GREAT and you look beautiful." Tim broke the silence that had hung comfortably in the living room. Aviva had removed her shoes and tucked her long legs underneath her when she joined him after putting Jenny to bed. She turned her gaze from the hearth to look at Tim.

He had fought throughout the evening to keep the mood light and celebratory, but he had been drawn again and again to her face and figure. In the firelight she looked like a madonna released from the confines of some ancient tapestry. The simplicity of her long-sleeved black dress only highlighted the uniqueness of her features, the voluptuousness of her body beneath the wool. It was fitting that she wore only a strand of simple pearls, for it was the beauty of the woman and not the dress that struck Tim. And her face—it was a study in contrasts.

The nose was long and aquiline; the mouth would have been considered a bit too wide on any other face. On hers the features flowed together in a mixture of strength and vulnerability. Her voice was bright and he hung on every word.

"You're just surprised to see me in something besides paint-covered jeans." Her long legs slipped to the floor as she stood up. "Can I get you some more brandy?" she asked lightly.

Before Tim could answer she had taken his snifter and crossed to the round table, which held the decanters, near the marble fireplace. Gracefully, she pulled the stopper from a decanter of Rémy Martin and poured the liquid into the glass. Buying time, Aviva held it for a moment over the candle flame to warm the drink.

"Mrs. Barber is moving in tomorrow. She decided she might as well not wait, since the place is finished." Aviva didn't turn to meet her young guest's eyes as she continued. "I just hope I haven't made a mistake allowing her to live here on a permanent basis. She's so..." Aviva groped for a word that didn't sound too harsh, "so eccentric."

"She can be a little strange at times, but I guess living alone in a big house for years will do that to a person," Tim agreed halfheartedly, his thoughts not on the old woman who was to be Aviva's first and lasting guest. Glancing over her shoulder, noting Tim's lack of interest, Aviva tried once more to get him involved in the subject of Gladys Barber and off the subject of Aviva Thompson.

"Strange!" She laughed, still twirling the glass over the flame, whose tongue reached for the crystal. "I'm not sure I have ever heard that woman say anything that didn't sound like an order or a complaint. I suppose it's partly her age, but I think she never lost that small-town biddyness. I understand she's from Missouri, or was years ago. You'd think she would have adopted some of the more casual attitudes of Californians. I mean, if she doesn't like it here, why doesn't she go back to the Midwest." Aviva swirled the glass faster, fully engrossed now in her one-sided conversation. "I hope she'll like everything here. I don't think I could take her constant complaining. Do you know that the last time I saw her she told me to get a woman in twice a week to watch the inn and Jenny so I could get away! She sounded like she owned Whaler's Inn and was ordering the help about. Perhaps she meant well, but she obviously doesn't understand how I feel about this place. Can you imagine ever wanting to leave even for a day?"

"Yes, I can." Tim's voice was low and firmly serious as he interrupted her stream of conversation. "I think it's a wonderful idea despite the way it was presented to you. After all, she can probably remember what it was like to be young and—"

"I doubt it." Aviva scoffed good-naturedly. "She must be at least ninety years old, and if she acted that way when she was young, I doubt whether she went anywhere at all—although Mr. Corbet says that she told him her husband was a real hell-raiser. I think when she moved here after he died, that's when she changed." Aviva couldn't help her tinkling laugh as she tried to imagine Gladys Barber young and married to a rake. The sound matched that of the crystal stopper being returned to the decanter.

Suddenly Tim was standing behind her and she could feel him almost reach out for her. Turning quickly, she handed him his drink and slipped out of his reach, settling herself back on the sofa before he could act.

"Aviva," he said, exasperation in his voice, "you can't live your whole life for Whaler's Inn. We both know it's been hard for you and that you've found some peace here, but you've got to realize that there's another life outside these walls. And if Gladys Barber drives you from this place for a day, a week, I'll say that she'll be a miracle worker."

Aviva heard the sense of what he was saying and the note of frustration in his usually calm, gentle voice. "What kind of life will it be for Jenny if her mother is cooped up here for twenty-four hours a day, three hundred and sixty-five days a year? It's not natural."

Aviva could feel the mounting friction. She swore quietly to herself. "A good life, Tim," Aviva answered truthfully, her voice soft as she tried to convey her determination. "I have made a decision to raise Jenny a certain way, but that doesn't mean that I don't want to live that way, too. I've worked hard for this—" her hand waved distractedly about her "—and, I intend to keep it for the two of us."

Tim stiffened at the obvious rejection, and Aviva

caught herself before her harsher thoughts became words. He would simply have to realize that their ideas of living were different and that she would not give him any hope. She was proud of what she had built, and her happiness did not depend on having a man around constantly, at least not Tim.

But looking at him, she couldn't help the sympathy that welled inside her. Even though she didn't want him for a lover, she certainly did for a friend. Yet she would not lead him on in order to keep that friendship.

"Tim," she said, "there are so many things you don't know about me. If you want to be my friend, that's wonderful. We already feel like you're part of the family, but beyond that, there is nothing." Setting her brandy snifter on the table, she stood up and stepped into her shoes.

"I have to check on Jenny." The wall had been gently but effectively placed between them and he was not given a chance to break it down before she glided out of the room.

Aviva stood in the entry hall listening to the last chime of the grandfather clock as it struck eleven. She reentered the living room after looking in on her sleeping daughter. The fire was almost out and the walls were patched by long shadows. Tim's tall, lanky frame melded with the phantasms. He spoke to her from across the room. She did not move from the doorway.

"Aviva, I know it's not the right time, but that wall can't stay up forever, and when it crumbles I'm going to be around to reach through and grab you before you fall with it."

They stood facing each other; there was nothing more to say. The words hung uneasily in the air. Aviva knew what courage it must have taken him to declare himself, and her heart went out to him. But his constant hope was almost maddening. She felt tired, the past year closing in on her. The worry of Jenny's future was enough for now. This man, this boy, was adding to the burden. Why couldn't he understand that?

As she continued to look at Tim, Aviva suddenly found herself wishing that Sam were with her. It would feel good to be next to him, to a man. A man with experience who could love her the way a woman should be loved, who understood her need to be cared for after all her hard work—the way she had tried to care for Sam after he had completed a commercial.

But the thought was simply a lacy, half-formed cobweb that Aviva found startlingly easy to brush away. It couldn't be, so there was no use worrying about it. She was on her own and that's the way things would stay. A soft sigh escaped her lips as she continued to watch the shadowy figure that was Tim.

The sound of the door bell chimes did not move them for a moment. They were suspended in time, each lost in parallel thoughts destined never to meet. It was hard for Aviva to move, she felt so tired. The chimes rang again, and summoning her energies, she crossed to the door, switching on the lights as she went.

The man's frame filled the doorway, the light catching his silver temples, dancing over the black waving hair above them. Aviva's hand came to her

mouth as she stifled a laugh. The man was impeccably
dressed. His European-cut tweed jacket skimmed his
tapered body and was buttoned over a stiffly starched
oxford cotton shirt and fawn-colored gabardine slacks.
It was the green-and-white plaid hat perched on the
back of his head that finally sent Aviva into a fit of
laughter.

"I'm terribly sorry. I seldom have that effect on
beautiful women." His eyes smiled at her as he strode
past her into the room. "I couldn't for the life of me
remember the name of this place. Diane said you
were just opening, but it finally came to me when I hit
Carmel."

Aviva recovered quickly from her mirth and, realizing the lateness of the hour and the fact that she
didn't know this man who had entered her home as if
he owned it, she was grateful that Tim still stood silently in the corner of the living room.

"I beg your pardon. You just took me by surprise.
Now, who are you and why are you here at this
hour?" Aviva asked incredulously as her new profes-
sional mind-set took hold. Her tone was terse and
businesslike.

"Don't tell me I'm your first?" He had turned with
his last words and was now examining her closely, obviously admiring the cut of her dress, the soft material
skimming her full-breasted figure, and her anger rose
at his innuendo. "Never let it be said that Jeremy
Crowley turned down the opportunity to be a first."
He extended a well-tanned hand that Aviva ignored.
Jeremy shrugged. "Diane did say that you were a little
different from the normal crowd."

"Diane? Diane who?" This conversation was not going at all well, and Aviva's frustration was rising.

"Diane Chesterfield, of course," the man answered, and Aviva blanched at the reference to the woman who had been a thorn in her side all the years she had lived in Los Angeles. Diane and her parties. Diane throwing herself at Sam. Diane, the epitome of the Los Angeles lady.

"Actually, I didn't know Diane very well." Funny, Aviva mused, since Sam had known the wild little lady all too well. "So I'm surprised that she was able to make a character judgment. Now, what was it she told you?"

"That your hotel was the place to stay. So here I am." He spread his arms out as if he expected her to fall into them, but Aviva stood her ground.

"Mr. Crowley, I'm afraid you'll be disappointed," she said curtly. "First, I'm surprised that Diane even knew I was opening an inn here in Carmel. Second, I'm afraid we don't officially open for business until tomorrow. You see, we just finished the renovations today and I'm afraid we're not ready for guests." As she spoke, Aviva realized that at the man's first appearance she had forgotten that the inn was more than her home.

"You mean it will be just you and me in this big house?"

Aviva's mouth fell open. She couldn't believe the way this person was speaking to her. This was just what she needed: a hotshot standing in her foyer and a lovesick boy in her living room. Not an auspicious beginning, she thought ruefully. Recovering her composure in an instant, Aviva opened her mouth to speak but before her sarcastic response could be made, Tim emerged from the shadows ready to defend Aviva against the stranger's impertinent, suggestive behavior.

"Mr. Crowley, perhaps Mrs. Thompson hasn't made herself clear. She is not ready for business. It's late and I think you had better go."

Jeremy stared at the young man, then turned his attention to Aviva, ignoring Tim completely.

"Look, I'm sorry but I've had a long drive and I always get a little hyper when I've spent an entire day pampering my clients and then taking to the road." His tone had softened but the rakish demeanor still remained. Remembrances of L.A. and Sam and people like the man in front of her flooded back into her mind and she felt herself begin to shiver. Strangely, though, she also seemed to enjoy the inexplicable electricity that emanated from him almost drawing her toward him. She felt light-headed. The brandy, she thought.

"I really do need a place to stay for the night, and, if it wouldn't be too much trouble, I'd like to stay here. It seems like the kind of place I'd be very comfortable in. Besides, it's late—where else am I to go?"

He did look tired, Aviva thought, despite the flashing smile and dancing black eyes. After all, with her bank account, how could she turn down a paying customer?

"It's all right, Tim." She sighed, feeling the younger man's resentment building. "Mr. Crowley might as well stay. It's only one night early and that's almost gone."

Aviva felt a slight tremor go through her body as both men continued to appraise her. It was late, and she knew this would be a good excuse to get rid of Tim gracefully, but for some reason she really didn't want to be left alone with this man who could conjure up her past so easily—all parts of her past.

"All right, Aviva, but..." Tim let his words trail off, the meaning was all too clear and the sentence didn't need to be finished.

"Thank you, Tim. We'll be fine." Aviva wished she felt as confident as her words sounded as she showed a reluctant Tim to the door and said her good-nights. Closing and bolting the door behind her, Aviva finally turned to face Jeremy Crowley.

"This way, if you don't mind," she said, squaring her shoulders as she walked by, indicating he should follow her to the desk.

By the time Jeremy Crowley had signed the register, Aviva had locked all the doors and turned off the hall lights. Joining her first guest on the landing, Aviva was aware that she must be extremely business-like in his presence. There was something about him that told her to be cautious. With dignity, Aviva led the way up the stairs, aware of his eyes on her back.

"This way, Mr. Crowley. My daughter's asleep in the west end of the house so, if you don't mind, I'm going to put you in the far east corner. The room is a bit feminine, but I'm sure you will be comfortable there."

Though her back was to him, she was conscious of

the pleasant odor of musk that surrounded him as she opened the heavy door and preceded him into the room.

"This is absolutely charming, Viva."

She bristled at his lack of respect in shortening her name. Yet from him, it did sound somehow pleasant. She berated herself harshly for such a silly thought and swore that she would never touch brandy again as long as she lived, knowing that it must be responsible for this deluge of ambivalent feelings.

"I'm sorry there's no wood for the fire," she continued, ignoring the familiarity of his speech. She wished he would stop staring at her as if he had never seen a woman before.

"Forget the firewood. I'm sure this hotel can get warm enough without it." His tone was playful and Aviva ignored the obvious innuendo. What nerve this man had! So like a friend of Diane's!

"I'll say good night then. Breakfast is at eight," she said curtly and turned to leave.

"Wait a minute, Mrs. Thompson." His voice was inviting even though there was a command buried in his tone. "If Diane recommended this place she must have known that I could find a good time here."

"I-I beg your pardon, Mr. Crowley?" Aviva stuttered, incredulous at the unspoken thought. She was frozen where she stood, unsure if she should be feeling the fear that was welling in her breast.

He came toward her. "You and Diane did travel in the same circles in L.A., didn't you?" he said, playing the word games that were so popular with the free-wheeling crowd he obviously seemed to run with.

This man thought she was the same kind of woman that Diane Chesterfield was! How dare he make that assumption—or that association! Anger now replaced concern, and she turned to face the man squarely, her fingers tightening around the brass doorknob as he continued to speak.

"Well, then, why don't we get some of that brandy I saw downstairs and get a little better acquainted." His voice was matter-of-fact as he made the suggestion. Obviously, he was used to having his way with women, and if Aviva had been honest, she would have admitted that it wouldn't be hard to become interested in such a man. "After all, as proprietor of this establishment you should be willing to show the hospitality of a true bed and board." He was closer now, and his scent assaulted her senses.

"I'm afraid you have mistaken Diane's recommendation. I don't play those games and I never have." Aviva's eyes blazed into his but Jeremy Crowley's gaze never faltered. The bright, white smile continued to flash at her.

"Good night, Mr. Crowley," she stated finally. But as she turned to go, her hand was suddenly captured, pressed under his as he halted her progress. Aviva glanced down at the hand covering hers. It was a strange sensation: the cold brass of the doorknob underneath her palm, the warmth of his hand on top. Was it shock or pleasure that shot through her body as she continued to stare at his masculine fingers? For a moment all thought was blocked from her mind. Then, looking back into his face, his eyes now frankly questioning hers, her green eyes hardened.

"You seem like an intelligent man, Mr. Crowley." Aviva's measured tone belied her confidence but she continued. "So use a little bit of that intelligence and never draw a conclusion about one person based on the idle chatter of another. Especially when that chatter comes from someone like Diane."

Sliding her hand from under his, Aviva turned, unhindered now, and left the room. In moments she was down the hall, thankful to be alone in her room with the door securely locked behind her. As she rested against the closed door, Aviva's eyes adjusted to the dark. Thoughts swirled and whirled about her mind but she could not seem to grasp them as they fluttered about her head. The only thing she was aware of was how beautiful the room looked in the moonlight. And how empty the bed.

Chapter Two

The first early morning light crept through the lace curtains by the canopied bed. Aviva had slept deeply, the sleep of total exhaustion and woken refreshed. For a minute she couldn't understand why she shouldn't feel as if the whole world were new, but a mental itch compelled her to remember the events of the night before. Alone in the high bed, she suddenly felt as if the down comforter was a weight she could not move as she lay, like a sweet prisoner, in its fluffy rose-colored confines. Her mind was now wandering freely back to the evening before.

The provocative Mr. Crowley was a carbon copy of Sam. Outrage churned inside her. Her anger was certainly directed toward him and his rude behavior but even more toward herself. How could she have allowed herself to be even slightly attracted to him?

Memories of the past year and a half yawned before her like some forbidding chasm suddenly illuminated. It was as if she hadn't learned anything from those experiences—the hurt her husband had brought her, the love for him that could never be reconciled, his death, the responsibility for her daughter, the inn. And now, the first man to touch her, to arouse her in any manner, was nothing more than an empty-headed playboy!

If she had thought, truly thought, Aviva would have acknowledged the glimmer of truth that sparkled deeply in her heart. She was only human and he was so much like Sam: physically attractive and confident. Her self-discipline had melted from the first moment he had touched her. The pragmatism and austerity that had ruled her personal life for so many months had been confronted by that ancient demon, pure desire, and Aviva was afraid to face the enemy.

"Mommy." Jenny's small hand covered her mother's, which lay limply on top of the satin quilt. "Are you okay? Are you sick?"

Aviva started, turned her head and looked into the little girl's concerned face. Her daughter's head barely reached the top of the high bed, and she stood on tiptoe to hold Aviva's hand. Aviva could feel the little body trembling as Jenny fought to keep her balance. Still no word came from Aviva. Her entire being was filled with such heartbreaking love that she felt it physically.

"Mommy?" Jenny questioned once again.

Aviva realized how silly her reminiscing was and immediately sprang up, throwing the comforter from her, one strap of her white silk gown slipping from her shoulder. Gathering up the child in one swift motion she brought her into the big bed and held her head gently to her warm breast.

"Everything will be fine," she whispered almost to

herself. The man down the hall would be out of her life in an hour just as Diane and Sam and all the rest of her old world were. Everything that was anything in the universe was in her room now, in the house she loved.

"No, my precious. Mommy was just thinking. I'm not sick. I'm wonderful and so are you!" The words tripped over each other as Aviva laid the little girl on the soft quilt and tickled her ribs until Jenny howled with delight.

"Mommy, you're tickling me too hard." Jenny screamed through her laughter and scampered to the other end of the bed as soon as she was released.

"So you can't take it, you rascal." Aviva teased as she readjusted the strap of her nightgown.

"Oh, yes I can." The defiant little chin pointed upward as Jenny challenged her mother. The little girl suddenly looked so serious that her mother laughed.

"What are you going to do today?" Aviva asked, "Well, what do you think?" Jennifer shrugged.

"I thought we might get up and make breakfast and then get Mrs. Barber's room ready. Can you help me with that?"

"Oh, sure, Mommy," Jenny said offhandedly before she continued. "Who was that man who came in last night?"

Aviva stiffened at the question. "How did you know someone came last night?" The silly drama of the past evening could not be forgotten, it seemed.

"I was awake and I heard him, and it wasn't Tim," Jenny answered.

"That was Mr. Crowley and he was our first

customer," Aviva answered, seeing no reason to go into a lengthy discussion. "But he's leaving this morning."

"Oh." Jenny's disappointment surprised Aviva.

"There's no need to look like a sourpuss, Jenny. Lots of people will come in and out of here all the time. Everybody has to leave here sometime, you know," Aviva gently scolded.

"Well, I just thought it would be fun to have somebody else around for a little bit. You and Tim are always working. I thought that man could play with me."

"Young lady, as assistant manager of this establishment, you cannot go around playing with the customers. Do you understand me?" Aviva tried to make a stern face but only caused Jenny to collapse in a fit of giggling once more. "Now, why don't you run along, get dressed and, if you need help tying your shoes or with your hair, you just come back, okay?"

Aviva closed the door slowly after Jenny and leisurely completed her morning toilette hoping that Mr. Jeremy Crowley had decided to leave early and not wait for breakfast. Finally, dressed in her best Saint Laurent jeans and a white silk blouse just in case any more unexpected guests dropped in, Aviva plaited her long hair and opened the door to the landing.

There on the floor outside her room lay a piece of the inn's stationery. Aviva picked it up, pleased at the sight of the beautiful oyster-gray paper but wondering how it got there. Turning it over she saw the note scrawled on the wrong side of the parchment.

I will need breakfast for two in my room at nine.
Jeremy Crowley

Her anger was instantaneous, rising to the surface like a long-dormant volcano suddenly brought to life by an unanticipated shifting of the earth beneath it. Aviva could feel the blood rushing to her cheeks. Her first thought was to storm into his room to find out who was with him. They had parted at midnight. How could he possibly have brought a woman into that room without her hearing them? How dare he bring her in without registering her? Besides that, he asked for a private breakfast. And what would he have done with his guest had Aviva accepted his thinly veiled proposition? It was unbelievable! The man's gall was beyond anything she had ever encountered. What kind of insensitive boor was he anyway?

Crumpling the paper she stormed down the three flights of stairs, hoping the noise would wake him from his miserable bed. Through her anger, though, she knew she couldn't afford to alienate him. After all, Diane had a lot of friends and Mr. Crowley probably did, too. They could both send her business she needed. But at that moment Aviva had her doubts about being an innkeeper.

Mercifully, her anger had turned to cold indifference by the time she began setting the tray with the delicate china. Every piece of breakage meant money out of her pocket, and she would not let Jeremy Crowley cost her a penny.

Finally the tray was ready: steaming coffee in a

silver pot, croissants, fresh melon balls in a crystal dish, cream, sugar. She had forgotten the juice. Prune, she decided, would do for both of them. The finishing touch was a sprig of lavender in a slim silver-and-crystal vase and two monogrammed peach linen napkins.

Carefully climbing the stairs, Aviva took a deep breath before she knocked resolutely on the door. Her lips were set in a thin line, hiding her anger, but presenting a far from friendly morning greeting.

"Come in, Mrs. Thompson." His deep voice sounded bright and cheery. No other sound came from the bedroom. Setting her jaw, Aviva opened the door, expecting a young nymph to appear from the bathroom at any moment clad only in his shirt. But it was not to be the sordid scene Aviva had imagined.

Her surprise was apparent as the lavender toppled from the tray she was trying desperately to balance. The other woman who greeted her was more of a shock than any she could have imagined. There, in the Queen Anne chair by the side of the bed, sat Jenny, her pudgy legs crossed at the ankles, elbows resting akimbo on the large arms of the chair. Jeremy Crowley was sitting up in bed, bare-chested, the covers drawn respectably up around his arms, the pillows piled high behind him.

"Hello, Mommy." Jenny greeted her mother as if her situation were the most natural in the world. "Jeremy and I have been waiting for our breakfast. He says you're late."

Aviva's mouth opened slightly as if to curtly answer her daughter; then she smiled reluctantly at the little girl. "I wouldn't have been late if someone would have told me that this was a very special breakfast indeed." She shot a reproachful look at the man in the bed, all the while smiling at her daughter. *No need to spoil her fun,* she thought as she moved toward the round table that stood between the bed and Jenny. Carefully moving the tulip-shaded lamp with one hand, Aviva set the tray down with the other.

"Now, first we'll let you two have a bit to eat and then, young lady, we'll discuss your behavior with our guest." Aviva could feel something happening behind her back and turned in time to see Jeremy signaling Jenny not to worry about her mother's scolding. She didn't like the idea that he had allowed Jenny into his room in the first place. After last night she was not at all sure she could even trust the man to be a paying guest at her inn.

Looking at him now though, his black hair tousled, the flecks of silver highlighting his temples, she could hardly believe that this was the same person who had advanced on her the evening before. He was so handsome, almost effervescent. His smile warmed the entire room on that gray, foggy morning. Aviva found herself smiling back at him, then, realizing this could be mistaken for consent to his shenanigans, she quickly drew her full lips back into the noncommittal line signaling an end to the fun.

"I'm sorry if Jenny disturbed you, Mr. Crowley," she said curtly.

"On the contrary, Mrs. Thompson, I was delighted when she came in to introduce herself. I haven't had such delightful female company in years, especially in my bedroom.'' His eyes sparkled at the statement and he seemed to drink in her form, which was amply displayed through the thin silk of her blouse and the fine cut of her denim jeans.

"Mr. Crowley, I would appreciate it if you would refrain from those kinds of comments while either Jenny or I are within hearing. I know the kind of people with whom you usually associate and this inn will not house many of them, I can assure you.''

Aviva wondered if she would regret this statement. He could provide a good trade for her bed and board. Shaking her head almost imperceptibly in response to her thoughts, she decided that it didn't matter if he never sent another guest to her hotel.

She had come to Carmel to escape his type. She had never catered to them when she was married to Sam and she wouldn't cater to them now. Turning on the heel of her tan brogues, she made her way to the door. His voice stopped her before she could reach it.

"Mrs. Thompson, I assure you I would never embarrass or harm your charming daughter, nor would I ever wish to bring you any distress.... I truly mean that. And, well, I do apologize for last night. Assumption is one of my major faults and I am very sorry. I can see now that you and Diane have very little in common.''

Aviva had always prided herself on her ability to read people, and her instinct told her that he was sincere. Sighing, she smiled reluctantly at him in acceptance of his apology.

"Thank you, Mr. Crowley.'' She left the room with a light warning to Jenny not to overstay her welcome.

Heading down the stairs, Aviva wondered why she didn't feel more relief that the man upstairs had seemingly withdrawn his attention so completely, so quickly.

Some feeling was stirring deep in the pit of her stomach. Was it disappointment? Perhaps being a desirable woman still held some meaning for her after all. Even if it did, though, she would never fulfill that need with someone like Jeremy Crowley, and it would be a long time before she ever gave it another thought.

"Hello!" A thin, commanding voice hailed her from the entry floor below, and she leaned over the carved oak railing to see Mrs. Barber waiting impatiently, surrounded by well-worn leather luggage and an ancient steamer trunk. The old woman stood, mopping her brow, her pink velvet hat slightly askew as she continued to call.

"Hello there," Aviva called from above.

"Finally, there you are," Gladys Barber called back. "I thought the house was empty."

Gritting her teeth against the woman's natural rancor, Aviva descended, composing herself as she went, wondering how she was going to deal with this salty old woman on a regular basis.

"I was wondering when you would show up." Aviva offered her a stunning smile when finally they stood facing each other, but the woman's unforgiving face left no room for pleasantries. All thoughts of Jeremy Crowley were pushed from her mind as she stood staring at her permanent boarder.

"You'll have to get the boy to help me; I'm afraid

you and I can't manage these alone." The little bird-like lady opened her coat to reveal a dark flowered shirtwaist dress. "Where is my room, now? You promised me the apple-green one with the French dressing table," the woman demanded. Aviva felt almost like a servant rather than the owner of Whaler's Inn every time Gladys spoke to her.

Aviva laughed, trying to make light of the situation. "First of all, there is no boy, but you just tell me which bags you need right away to settle in, and I'll bring them up to your room now. I'll attend to the others later. Now, just go up to the first landing; your room is the only one there, so it should be very quiet."

"No boy!" Mrs. Barber muttered as she pointed to the two oldest cases and then proceeded slowly up the stairs. "How are you going to manage to care for this place with no boy, what with that little girl of yours?"

Aviva shook her head, a heavy sigh escaping her lips as she looked at the woman who walked ahead of her. Mrs. Barber was a godsend, she had to admit. The woman was well-known in Carmel, and her decision to move into Whaler's Inn permanently was considered a sort of local blessing, but Aviva had a feeling that it might be a curse, too. Mrs. Barber's curt manner and what seemed to be constant complaints might prove to be more trouble than she was worth. If only she had been a sweet, plump, grandmotherly type who could keep Aviva company on the cold winter nights ahead. Ah, well, nothing to do about it now. Aviva needed the money and she could put up with anything to make Whaler's Inn and her new life work the way she wanted them to.

Thankfully, Mrs. Barber had seemed absolutely delighted with the room. The crisp apple-green of the bed coverlet was offset by the sheer organdy dust ruffle and balloon shades over the bay windows. A spindle-back rocking chair with a shell-pink cushion sat by the fireplace, a large wool-gathering basket beside it.

Aviva had remembered everything, including the woman's love of heirloom snuff bottles. The younger woman had placed two beautiful bottles on the dressing table to add to Gladys's collection in the hope of softening her just a bit.

After lighting the fire, Aviva had withdrawn to attend to her duties in the kitchen and all about the large house. With Mrs. Barber settling in, she somehow felt that all was right. More than likely the older woman would keep to herself and not be a bother to Aviva at all. At least that was the little prayer Aviva muttered to herself as she went about her chores.

Soon, she knew, each of the rooms would be filled and there would be croissants and coffee for twenty-four people each and every day of the year. Maybe Gladys Barber was a good-luck boarder. But, more than likely, the ads Aviva had placed in the travel sections of the important California newspapers would do the trick.

She would need someone to help out, though, if Whaler's Inn did catch the fancy of the traveling public. Aviva decided to check into the possibility of part-time help during her next trip into Carmel. Looking about the big house, she feared she would never set foot in town again with all the cleaning that had to be done.

It was almost noon when Jenny and Jeremy appeared at the kitchen door. Aviva was ashamed to admit it, but she had all but forgotten her daughter. In Carmel one could do that. There was nothing that could harm a child. And after the morning apology, Aviva had few reservations about the company Jenny had chosen to keep.

"So, where have you two been? I hope you haven't been bothering Mr. Crowley, Jenny. He probably has to be on his way soon." Aviva wiped her floured hands on her apron after giving the bread dough she was kneading one final pat. A gentle hint never hurt, and the sooner he left the better.

"Actually, Mrs. Thompson..." Aviva looked up and smiled. He must have realized that she preferred to be addressed formally. "I was wondering if I might be able to extend my stay. Now that you're officially open, of course." His smile was so open, his face so fresh and alive and wholesome, that Aviva wondered if she had only dreamed of his insolence.

"I wouldn't hesitate if I were you," he continued quickly. "The first lesson of good business is to capitalize on your opportunities, and it looks as if this would be a wise course of action."

"Of course, of course," Aviva answered. "I don't know why I even hesitated. I'll simply add the time to your bill." Quickly, she turned her eyes back to the bread, ashamed of the blush that was creeping over her. After all, she thought, when the lady doth protest too much, trouble is always invited, and there was no money in the till. Besides, he didn't seem so bad in the first light of day, and he was obviously entranced by Jenny. There must be a gentleman hidden inside him.

"I'm glad to hear that. I can really use a few days out here in God's country. Do you mind if I use the phone to call my office?"

"No, the charge will also be on your bill." Aviva smiled sweetly, proud of her one-upmanship, as she beckoned toward the alcove in which the phone sat.

"I think you're going to have one heck of a success on your hands with that kind of thinking, Aviva Thompson." Jeremy chuckled as he made his way to the hall to make his call.

He was gone only minutes and spoke immediately upon returning to the warmth of the kitchen. "Now, could I persuade my two new friends to accompany me to lunch in town? I really would like to make amends." His dark eyes were sincere, his voice polite as he extended the invitation. Aviva raised her eyes to meet his, smiling warmly for the first time since he had walked through her door.

"Thank you for the offer. I do appreciate your intent, but there is simply too much to do and no one to look after the inn if someone should come by." She hoped that he understood her sincerity, but the idea was impossible. Aviva recognized the personal threat he posed and she would make every attempt to keep herself from compromising situations. She was not going to make a fool of herself over a man who would be at Whaler's Inn for only a few days. And beyond that, of course, there could be nothing. As charming as he may seem in the old house in Carmel, Aviva knew only too well what his life in Los Angeles must be like and she would never want any part of that.

"What do you mean no one here!" Aviva was startled out of her thoughts at the clipped words that rang through the kitchen. "Who do you think I am?"

All eyes turned toward Mrs. Barber, who walked determinedly into the room. "Why, I could look after everything and probably do a better job with that bread than you can. Hello, young man," she continued, turning her attention to Jeremy as she extended her thin, blue-veined hand. "I don't believe we've met. I'm Gladys Barber and I live here."

"So nice to meet you. I live here, too. But only for a few days, unless the chill here at Whaler's Inn thaws a bit. If that happens, I may extend my stay." He shot a teasing glance at Aviva, who turned away and kneaded her bread with renewed vigor. Mrs. Barber didn't even try to pretend to ignore the comment but laughed a dry laugh behind her dainty fingers.

With each knead Aviva found herself becoming angrier that a man she didn't even know and a woman who was, after all, only a boarder seemed to be ganging up on her. This was not at all how she imagined her first days as an innkeeper!

"Are those your bags I saw in the hall?" Jeremy continued to address the old woman.

"Yes, they are. Would you help me up the stairs with them? I'm sure Aviva could never manage it by herself and—" she leaned forward whispering conspiratorially but still loud enough for Aviva to hear "—you know, there is no boy yet." Jeremy looked shocked and drew back as if aghast.

"Well, in that case I'll have to carry them up myself

and then you and Jenny and I will leave Mrs. Thompson to carry on with her household chores while the three of us go to lunch. Of course, we can only go if we have her permission." He looked at Aviva, his eyes soulful, like an old hound she had once seen in a Mickey Rooney–Judy Garland movie.

He's too much, Aviva thought, exasperated by his behavior but amused at the same time. At least he didn't complain like Gladys! Well, Jenny couldn't go, of course. Breakfast was one thing but—

"Young man," Gladys broke in before Aviva could decline the invitation for Jenny, "I'm well above the age of consent, so I don't need the lady of the house to tell me where I can and cannot go, and I'm sure she would dearly love to have Jenny out from underfoot for a few hours. Wouldn't you, dear?"

Aviva's mouth fell open. How that woman was taking over! It was beyond belief! She looked from one person to the other: Jenny standing quietly by Jeremy's legs, Mrs. Barber daring her to forbid the outing knowing that Jenny would be terribly upset if she did, and Jeremy Crowley viewing the entire proceeding with total amusement.

"All right, all right," Aviva finally relented. Anything to get them all out of her hair for a little while. "But Mrs. Barber, you be sure to keep an eye on Jenny. Sweetheart, you go upstairs and get your jacket. It's going to be cold today."

"Okay," Jenny and Jeremy said in unison as he swept the little girl up into his arms and headed for the stairs, both of them laughing uproariously as they went.

"You thought Mommy called you sweetheart!" Aviva could hear Jenny's giggle as they disappeared from sight.

"Nice young man." Gladys Barber touched Aviva's arm conspiratorially.

Aviva looked down at the little woman and simply sighed in response. What was the use? She did admit that he was a charming man but she wasn't going to say it out loud. And she certainly wasn't going to admit it to Gladys Barber, who seemed to want to be included in every thought Aviva had or every action she took.

More than likely Gladys had been alone so long she didn't remember all the trouble men could cause. Immediately, Aviva berated herself for thinking poorly of Gladys, who probably had been alone an awfully long time. She would have to be more understanding with the woman even though she did poke her nose where it didn't belong.

But Gladys would not release Aviva's arm until she gave some sort of answer. "Yes, he is a nice man, Mrs. Barber, but he's just a guest. And one who seems to become familiar far too fast for my tastes." Aviva hoped that the two-pronged message would somehow penetrate Gladys's psyche, but instead, the woman simply shrugged at what she considered to be a highly satisfactory answer and left Aviva alone.

Surprisingly, as the afternoon wore on, Aviva found herself actually thinking extra-kind thoughts about Jeremy Crowley. It *had* been nice having the whole day to herself. Two reservations had been made for the following week—both for extended stays—the house was spotless, dinner was almost ready, and she still had time to bathe and dress before dinner. She would need to be relaxed if Gladys decided to complain about the food, too.

Slowly she made her way about the house, checking on the smallest details, running her hands lovingly over the dark wood that seemed to sparkle under the lights she now switched on for the evening. As she climbed the stairs to her room, she knew she would have to look into the possibility of getting help the very next day.

When Aviva heard the car drive up, she ran to the window, gathering her robe about her as she went. Throwing open the window, she saw the threesome climb out of the car and head for the back door.

"Hey," she cried, leaning over the sill, "you'll have to go around the front. I locked the back door. Dinner's in an hour, so hurry and get cleaned up." Aviva closed the window against the chill and hurried to dress so that she could receive her guests as a proprietress should.

The conversation over drinks was pleasant as they all sat in the drawing room waiting for the dinner to finish cooking. Jenny had done an admirable job getting ready all by herself, but her barettes needed a little attention.

As the little girl stood quietly waiting for her mother to finish, Aviva was aware of Jeremy's eyes on her even though he kept up a constant stream of conversation with Mrs. Barber, who was unusually docile. She hoped her dress for the evening meal was right.

In an effort to completely dispel Jeremy's pre-
conceived notion of her character, she had dressed
demurely in a high-necked antique satin-and-lace
blouse, a simply cut black velvet skirt and low-heeled
patent pumps, adorned only with small grosgrain
bows. She had carefully arranged her heavy hair in a
chignon at the nape of her neck. Far from achieving
the schoolmarm appearance she desired, Aviva had
transformed herself into a nineteenth-century beauty
and Jeremy could not take his eyes off her.

Jenny provided the conversation over the beef Stro-
ganoff dinner and continued her chatter about golf
through the chocolate mousse. Jeremy, it seemed,
was quite an expert on the subject and had treated his
two dates to a trip to the world-renowned Pebble
Beach club. Aviva was proud of her bright little girl.
Jeremy only corrected her once, when she referred to
a divot as a drivot.

As the last spoonful of rich mousse was devoured,
Aviva interrupted Jenny's discussion of the rich
man's game of golf. "Jenny, I think it's time you
headed off to bed." The little girl replied by screwing
her face into a little ball.

"None of that, now. Off you go. I'll come up and
tuck you in after I clean the dishes." Jenny hopped
down from the high mahogany chair and slowly
walked out of the dining room without another word.

"Now," she said, turning her attention to the two
adults at the table, "would you like to have your coffee in the living room while I clean up the table?"

"That would be nice, dear," Gladys answered roy-
ally. "Will you join us?" Obviously the dinner had

improved Gladys's disposition and Aviva smiled at her, forgiving her tone, as Jeremy helped her from her chair and linked his arm through hers.

"Thank you, but you forget I'm not a guest. Go ahead and I'll serve your coffee in a minute. There's brandy in the decanter by the fireplace." Aviva cleared the table, softening a bit toward Gladys as she did so, reminding herself that it was just the old woman's way, even if she didn't like it. After settling her guests with their coffee, Aviva returned to the kitchen while they settled down to a quiet chat.

It had been a truly enjoyable evening, and she felt more comfortable with Jeremy Crowley as a person. But as a man, he still caused her a great deal of discomfort. It seemed he never took his eyes off her for a minute.

Finally, all the dishes and crystal were cleaned and sparkling. She had laid out the breakfast china, napkins and trays for the following day, hoping to gain a little time in order to find a way to get into town to hire some help.

After pouring herself the last cup of coffee, she passed through the swinging door that divided the kitchen from the dining room. Aviva cocked her head. All was quiet in the living room, and the soft glow of light indicated the fire was dying. It would seem, she thought, that everyone was exhausted from the day's outing and had gone to bed. Just as well; she really didn't feel like company. It would be wonderful to sink into one of the deep wing chairs and kick off her shoes while she had her coffee alone.

Aviva made her way toward the living room to put

her cup down before she went to kiss Jenny good-night. She did not consider turning on a light; she knew the house as if she had lived there all her life. Suddenly she stopped short. Jeremy Crowley was still there, sipping his brandy, staring into the dying fire.

"You startled me." Aviva approached and placed the dainty cup on the low table between them. "I thought everyone had turned in early."

In the half light she could barely see his face. But somehow she felt that she had stumbled onto the real Jeremy Crowley. Gone was the jolly, teasing man who had appeared at her door the night before. There was no trace of the fast-moving L.A. businessman. Even the child charmer had retired for the evening. Here in the soft light he was subdued, thoughtful. Aviva liked this man who sat nestled in the deep chair.

"I was waiting for you, hoping we might be able to have a talk. I really do want you to know that I feel terrible about the way I acted when we met. I know that to say I had a lot on my mind is no excuse, but I did. And sometimes it's hard to stop the playacting, hard to remember I'm not running like a crazy man down the streets of Beverly Hills. I would appreciate it very much if we could start again as friends. Please."

Friends! What a surprising word for him to use. She would like to be his friend but she knew that it could easily turn into so much more. It was dangerous—the idea of being his friend—but also tantalizing.

"It's all right, really it is. I lived your type of life long enough. I had just forgotten what it was like. Things are so quiet and simple here. It's hard to imagine anyone would enjoy the way you must live."

"You might be right, but, well, most of us have never had the courage to do what you've done: just leave it behind." He was looking at her as he spoke, but she couldn't see his eyes. "You know, if you think about it," he continued before she could speak, "I'll bet even you could remember a few good times you had back there. After all, life is only what you make of it. It doesn't have to be a rat race twenty-four hours a day."

"I suppose not," Aviva admitted reluctantly. It did seem hard to believe that those who had money and power, which Jeremy obviously seemed to have, wouldn't always lead a fast life. "I can remember some very good times. It's just that even those weren't as good as what I have here."

"Really?" The question was not impertinent but it somehow grated on Aviva. How could he even question what she was saying? He had only been at Whaler's Inn for a day. She had spent a year slaving to make it what it was, getting to know her neighbors. Of course it was better.

"Well, don't knock it until you've tried it," Aviva said somewhat too quickly as she rose from her seat. "I have to go up and tuck Jenny in. But by now I imagine she'll be fast asleep. I'll be back in a moment if you'd still like to have some company now that we're friends." Aviva was grateful for the dark. She knew if he could see her face he would easily have read the confusion she was feeling.

"Aviva." His voice stopped her, and she turned her head, looking back over her shoulder at the shadowy figure, not noticing that he had used her first name—

it seemed so familiar. "Would you like to bring a coat down with you? Perhaps we could go for a walk?"

"That would be nice. Be back in a minute." Without exactly knowing why, she floated up the stairs. Jenny was asleep, so she kissed her, tucking the quilt on the small bed under her pouting chin. Grabbing the first jacket she could lay her hands on, Aviva went back down to the entry where Jeremy awaited.

Jeremy suffered from the damp, chill air more than Aviva as they walked down the dark road toward Carmel. After so many months in the area, she had become immune to the penetrating chill. To their left, they could hear the pounding of the ocean, all around them the creaking of the trees.

Aviva felt invigorated as the wind whipped her hair loose from the tortoise pins that held it. The conversation was light and she felt alive.

"Did you know that the stars actually rule your life?" Jeremy had quipped, raising one strong hand toward the sky.

"Oh, really. I didn't know you were an astrologer," Aviva had teased back.

"Hardly" was his only answer. Aviva's interest was piqued.

"Well, then, what are you?"

"I'm a mad scientist working on a new drug that will have beautiful women worshiping at my feet, and you have been chosen to be my first victim." Aviva offered a wry smile as Jeremy chuckled at his own joke. Casting her a glance, he shrugged his shoulders comically. "Actually, that's a lie."

"No kidding?" came her sarcastic comment.

"I'm a developer. Shopping centers, business offices..." The rest was lost to the wind but Aviva didn't mind. She could just imagine the wheeling and dealing that went on in his world. Not much different from Sam's commercials, she thought, trying to push aside the sadness that she suddenly felt.

"I guess it's not terribly interesting," Jeremy said quickly noting her lack of interest.

"Oh, I'm sure it is," she answered politely.

"Well, a job is a job, isn't it?" he offered, trying to make amends—for what, he wasn't sure. They walked on in silence for a few moments, Jeremy stuffing his hands deeper in the pockets of his jacket against the cold.

"You know, though, there are some things that are really wonderful. Like your daughter. If I had a daughter I'd want one just like Jenny. She's a great kid." In the dark, Aviva blushed with pleasure. She was happy when other people thought Jenny special.

"You don't have any children, then?" she pressed, suddenly curious about his personal life.

"No. Never been married. Never had the pleasure of fathering a child." Even with the wind she could hear the wistful tone in his voice. Even in the dark she could see the faraway look in his eyes, and her heart went out to him.

"I see" was all she could think to say.

"Not that I've given up hope, mind you." Jeremy shook his finger at her and instinctively she believed him. "I intend to have it all someday. When the time is right. In fact, maybe the stars will tell me how soon that will be." He looked up into the sky and began to make up the most outrageous stories, and Aviva laughed, forgetting all about his Beverly Hills job but remembering his desire for a family. She tucked the information away in her heart and then attended to his stories.

As they walked and talked and laughed and then were silent, Aviva was not even aware that she no longer compared Jeremy to Sam or worried about where he came from and what he did when he was firmly ensconced in Los Angeles. It was good to talk with a man again. Better, now that her confidence as a businesswoman was so high. The year working on Whaler's Inn had provided her with much more than a beautiful hotel. It had allowed Aviva to grow in a way she had never thought possible.

Oh, the transition had been slow. In fact, barely perceptible. She had not even acknowledged the change. No longer was she afraid to face life. No longer was she wary of the future. Her shoulders were carried a little squarer, her speech was more secure. The escape she thought she had sought had become a haven. The pleasure of accomplishment now allowed her to face a challenge as a person, not as the wife of a philandering husband or the mother of a young, beautiful daughter. Perhaps the newfound confidence even allowed her to enjoy Jeremy now as she had thought she would never enjoy the company of a man again.

They laughed in unison when the wind rose and cut off their conversation for a moment or two as they strolled slowly along the beach. Finally, after twenty minutes of fighting the elements, Aviva suggested resting. Instinctively, grabbing his hand as a friend would, she led him off the road and onto the sand. Then she motioned him to sit behind one of the dunes that would protect them from the wind.

He had hesitated when she started to draw her hand from his. Her body stiffened as she felt the pressure of his fingers. Seeming to understand her uncertainty without knowing its source, he released her. The silence of their retreat seemed to infect them, and the banter had died with the howling of the wind.

Finally he spoke, asking a question for which Aviva did not consciously have the answer. "I don't really understand you. One moment you're an efficient modern woman, the next a prim and proper Victorian lady. Who are you really?"

Aviva tipped her head to the sky, the moon casting an aura about her profile. She appeared to look to the stars for an answer. Her heart knew what she wanted to say, but tonight her mind would not form the words. She wanted to try to explain herself to Jeremy.

"There's nothing to understand." Her voice carried through the cold night air. "I'm really quite a simple woman."

There was something in the way she said this that stopped his protest. Jeremy waited, unmoving, for her to continue.

"You see, I love the stars but I don't want to be one except in Jenny's eyes. The life I lived before wasn't mine, it was my late husband's. I want Jenny to know what it's like to live where you can see blue sky, not smog. A place where people are kind to each other because they like one another, not because of what they can get." She turned back to him, searching his shadowed face for any sign of understanding, but he had simply melted into the dunes, a sand statue to whom she could verbalize her feelings without reprisal. He was not truly real, so she felt at ease. "Do you know that most children in Southern California don't know what the seasons are? I want Jenny to rejoice in the warmth of sunshine after a cold winter. Do you see?" she asked, almost pleading for his understanding.

"In a way. But what about you?" he asked softly.

"Me? I want all those things for myself, too. It's so comforting living in a place like this." Even to Aviva the statement sounded hollow—not at all communicating the fullness of life she felt she could live in Carmel.

As she waited for him to speak, Jeremy moved, shifting to rest on his knees, his hands placed lightly on his well-formed thighs. "And what about the other kind of comfort?" She looked at him, silently questioning as he continued. "The kind that not only comforts the soul but the heart and body? The kind a man can give you?"

The silence stretched to breaking as Aviva considered her answer; then she spoke. "Truthfully, Jeremy, I don't know. There has been so much to do for such a long time." It was a simple statement; there was no self-pity, no bitterness anymore.

Jeremy, touched by the strength of her words, reached out his large, smooth hands and took hers. Without knowing if she wished it or not, her body was drawn gently toward his until they were kneeling before each other on the cool sand.

Releasing her left hand, he reached up to touch her face, sweeping an errant strand of hair back behind her delicate ear, gently, so he wouldn't frighten her. His square-tipped fingers continued to search as a blind man's would, exploring her smooth brow, outlining her straight nose and full lips. She did not move; there was no response without or within. It was as if she had quietly stepped out of her body and was thoughtfully watching the couple on the sand to see how the woman would behave, whether she would shudder with delight or cry out from the surprise and shock of such tenderness after so long.

Suddenly, she felt the urgency in him as both his hands slipped around the back of her head and he pulled her face to his, tipping it to place his lips exactly over hers. His kiss was gentle, an extension of the now-quiet breeze that played about them, harboring a passion as yet unknown. His body leaned into hers, breast almost touching breast. Then she was no longer a spirit watching with detached interest.

It started slowly: a breeze that quickly became a whirlwind of desire in her body. She began to respond to the insistent kiss. Her arms were torn from her sides and flung about his neck, pulling him ever closer until the two became one. But even as she relished the physical closeness, Aviva's mind rebelled, calling out to nature to stop the insanity while she could. She began to move in his arms. Not in pleasure as he did, but with final decision not to let this continue, though even as she struggled she knew her heart was being lost to him.

Jeremy held her tighter, unwilling to let her slip

from his grasp. "Aviva, don't," he whispered as his lips left hers and his smooth cheek pressed into the mass of hair that now cascaded about her shoulders.

With a calm strength she didn't know she possessed, she pushed her body from his. Her breathing was labored but her eyes were clear, her head held high.

"No," she said firmly, her words piercing the night, "I simply am not ready to give anything to you—any kind of love." Gracefully, reluctantly, she raised herself from the sand and looked down on him, her face covered by the darkness and a shadow of regret as if she knew she might be closing the door on something as good and wonderful as she had ever known in her life. But she turned on her heel and made her way back to the inn. It was in the kitchen that Jeremy found Aviva, meticulously washing the cups from which they had been drinking before their walk. For a minute he stood, silently contemplating the back of her, then he spoke.

"Aviva." Her head turned; she had not been frightened by his sudden presence. He felt sure that she was a woman rarely frightened and then only with good reason. "I want you to know that I have time."

She studied his face as he spoke to her, then smiled a warm and open smile. "I appreciate that, Jeremy. I truly do. But we'll see. Time is a funny thing."

"Well, then, for now good night, Mrs. Thompson."

"Good night, Mr. Crowley." Turning back to the sink, Aviva smiled to herself. She would sleep well that night.

Chapter Three

True to his word, Jeremy allowed her time during the next few days. His advances were gentle; a tender, understanding smile, a simple act of tying Jenny's shoes did not go unnoticed. Strangely, it was as if the whole world had suddenly added 200-watt bulbs to their lamps. Despite the heavy fog that intermittently blanketed the coast, the world was brighter, lighter, and Aviva felt herself craving more and more of Jeremy's company.

When he was out—golfing, or whatever kept him busy during the day—she found she missed his mere presence. But there was always a reminder: a book left by the fireplace, his silly green hat perched on the bedpost in his room when she went to clean, and everywhere the scent of him.

But then, each night, no matter how late she finished her work, he would be there for her. It had become a ritual: the coffee on the table, a fire lit and blazing, the conversation good, safe and interesting. Sometimes he would read to her, and she realized that it had been years since she had even held a book. The fabulous images of Lawrence, the strange sultriness of Fitzgerald and the curious banality of the people Updike wrote about entranced her. But always, there was a joke, a witticism that ended their conversations, and more often than not, the play on words was directed toward himself—a trait that endeared him to Aviva. And she was content. She would even admit to being happy had she been asked.

Happy in more ways than one. Several more guests had arrived and Aviva thanked her lucky stars that the advertising that had seemed such an extravagance was working. One or two people were going to stay a few days, the others for only a night; this gave the inn the feeling of activity, normalcy, success. Those guests left pleased with the service at the quiet, quaint inn, promising to tell their friends about it. Life seemed so right.

A girl from town now came to help in the early-morning and the evening hours. She was nice but somewhat simple. Her farm-girl bulk made her perfect for carrying guests' luggage up and down the long flights of stairs and her quiet, gentle demeanor allowed her to happily complete the chores about the kitchen and the bedrooms. No one, not even inquisitive Jenny, seemed to take much interest in her. In fact, only Aviva could remember her name those first few days. So she moved about the house like some benign spirit accomplishing her everyday tasks. Aviva could now retire to her own room each afternoon to nap or play with Jenny or hope that Jeremy would appear.

It was Wednesday before she knew it, and suddenly

Aviva realized that Jeremy would be on his way soon, long before she was ready to let him leave. As she stood preparing dinner for the evening meal, she found herself lost in the daydream of what her evenings would be like without him. The potato peeler stopped midair, her green eyes stared out the window toward the beach but did not really see it. There would be seven for dinner that evening but she could think of little else than Jeremy's departure.

So lost was she in her thoughts that she didn't even hear the phone ringing in the alcove just past the dining room. It wasn't until Gladys charged through the kitchen door that Aviva turned her attention back to the utensil, pretending not to have heard Gladys's entrance.

"You should open your ears," the old woman announced as she came to stand by Aviva.

"What?" Aviva turned a calm face toward Gladys.

"The telephone. It's Tim, for you." Gladys made no move to leave after her message was delivered, so Aviva wiped her hands on her apron and spoke before turning toward the door.

"Mrs. Barber..." she began.

"You ought to be calling me Gladys by now," the old woman ordered curtly.

Aviva lowered her eyes and counted to ten, realizing that Gladys meant no harm with her harsh way of speaking. She herself had to be more patient, that was all.

"All right, Gladys." She made the effort, cringing slightly, hoping that the woman wouldn't take it as a sign to include herself even more in the everyday goings on of the inn and Aviva's life. "You really shouldn't have to bother yourself with things like answering the phone. That's what Sue is here for, or me. You're supposed to be a guest."

"Well, if I didn't do it no one would have. You didn't hear it ringing and Sue is upstairs doing the beds. She doesn't have time to come running down here, and you told her not to use the phone in your room." Gladys mumbled all the way out the door, and for a minute Aviva thought that she had possibly hurt the woman's feelings. Dismissing the thought, knowing that Gladys was far too crusty for such a simple thing to have that effect, Aviva followed her through the kitchen door and picked up the phone.

"Hi," she said evenly, not letting Gladys get her down. Tim was happy as a clam, having just finished a project that had taken up most of his time for the past month or so. His good humor infected Aviva, and she was soon chatting away about the last window that Tim had promised to do for the inn. It was a very small project, half hidden in the stairwell, but Aviva knew she wouldn't rest until Whaler's Inn was perfect.

Feeling magnanimous, Aviva invited Tim to join them for dinner that night, even though the table would be fuller than usual, then hung up and went to finish peeling the vegetables. Again, she found herself staring out the window, and she berated herself for her silliness, trying desperately to keep her mind on the job at hand.

It was funny how a man who had disturbed her so much on their first meeting could now become the focal point of her thoughts. But Jeremy was, and there seemed little she could do about it.

Finally finishing with the vegetables, she put them in a large pot, covered them with cold water, and was about to wash the sink out when she noticed a lone figure walking in the field near the beach. Upon closer inspection she was almost sure it was Jeremy. The height of the man, the black hair, the way he carried himself—it was Jeremy. What was he doing out there in the field, she wondered.

Mesmerized, she continued to watch as the figure bent now and then as though examining the terrain. Slowly he came closer until Aviva could see that it certainly was Jeremy Crowley taking a leisurely walk in the middle of the day.

Funny, she had never really considered what he did with his days. Could it be that the man who drove the Mercedes, the man whose clothes looked as if they came right off Rodeo Drive in Beverly Hills, actually enjoyed taking nature hikes? How full of surprises he was.

As she watched him come closer and closer, Aviva felt her body take over as her mind allowed itself to simply enjoy the sight of him. Could this be she? This woman whose pulse beat faster even though wood and brick, glass and land separated her from a man she hardly knew? Could the merest glint of foggy sunlight dancing off his hair make her mouth just a bit dry, her eyes glisten as they hadn't for months—no, years?

Now he was almost close enough to see her from where he stood, and Aviva quickly turned away from the window, somehow afraid that he would see the rush of blood coming to her cheeks or know instinctively what she was thinking about him, about herself.

To her embarrassment the blush had not subsided when she heard the sound of the back door open and Jeremy enter. Luckily Aviva's head was buried in the refrigerator and she pretended not to hear him. But when she saw the toes of his shoes directly under her eyes, it was even more foolish not to acknowledge his presence.

"Something for the proprietress of Whaler's Inn," he said, smiling his dazzling smile as he handed her a bunch of wildflowers.

Aviva straightened herself and accepted the flowers, unable to keep the surprised look from her face. So it wasn't a nature hike. He had actually been out picking flowers for her. Unfortunately, it really wasn't the time of year for wildflowers, and Aviva seemed to be holding a handful of weeds. But it was the thought that counted, and she was more touched than words could express.

"Thank you, they're..." What was the word? "They're lovely, Jeremy."

"I know that they're not exactly centerpiece flowers, but it was the best I could do out there." His grin seemed to ignite a spark somewhere deep inside her, and she turned quickly away from him with the excuse that she would find a vase. The truth was, she had to get away from him. A few inches, a few feet, it was amazing how distance did nothing to ease the excitement that began to stir the moment he came into a room.

"Well," Jeremy asked, lounging against the refrigerator door Aviva had just closed, "how am I doing?"

"Doing at what?" Aviva asked, laughing over her shoulder at him. "As a flower picker I would have to say honestly that I think you need more practice." Oh, how she would miss his gentle, surprising ways, she suddenly thought as she finished her sentence.

"How am I doing with the lady of this house?" he said, suddenly serious. "I've used up almost all the tricks I know. I've read poetry, utilized the fine art of conversation, spent my morning picking flowers. Are my charms working at all?"

"The lady of the house appreciates all the attentions that have been paid to her," Aviva answered lightly, trying to recapture the feeling of humor. She didn't want to talk seriously with him, afraid that she might start considering him as a man, a lover, if she did. It was fine to have fleeting fancies about him in her own mind but she didn't want to take a chance on letting him know that his attentions had affected her greatly.

Jeremy took a few steps in her direction and instinctively Aviva drew back. He stopped, his eyes full of questions, even reflecting a little hurt. But he recovered almost instantaneously, his natural resilience coming to the surface. "I mean it, Aviva. I really want to know."

Insistence always made Aviva nervous, and this instance was no exception. She knew she had to answer him, but choosing the words was extremely difficult. They had to mean exactly the right thing. "And I meant what I said. I truly have appreciated your company, loved your company, Jeremy. It's been a long time since someone has been able to take my mind completely off this risky business I chose and to enter my—" She stopped speaking. She was going too far.

"Yes?" He urged her on.

"My personal life," she finished, her tone indicating that there was to be no more discussion.

Jeremy knew she had no desire to talk about her private life. He had tried to get her to open up so often during their long evenings together but she would have none of it. Today, she was not going to be so lucky.

"Aviva, haven't we been friends long enough to have a serious talk? I'm getting a little tired of Fitzgerald. What I really want to know is all about you and Jenny, what you did in Los Angeles before you came here—"

"Jeremy," Aviva cut him off, twisting the towel she was holding in her hands. "I'm sorry, but I thought I had already made myself clear on that point. I have really enjoyed your company. More than you'll ever know, but I really don't want to discuss it."

"Okay." He held up his hands, calling a truce. There would come another time, he knew. Reaching out, he dunked his hand into the cold water in the pot and grabbed a carrot.

"You don't mind, do you?" he asked, indicating the carrot that was already disappearing into his mouth.

Aviva shook her head. "Just don't eat too many or you won't be able to have any with dinner."

"Oh, I am sorry, Aviva. I should have told you I

won't be here for dinner. I have an engagement this evening.''

Hurt flooded over her. It was the first time since he had arrived at the inn that he had not spent the evening with her. If she didn't count the first night, of course. She wasn't really surprised at her feelings. He had become more and more important to her as each day passed. She was just a little angry that her reactions were so immediate. After all, there was nothing between them—not for his lack of trying. She had chosen it to be that way. To cover up her feelings, she turned away and busied herself cleaning the counter she had already cleaned.

"That's all right," she answered, trying to keep her voice even. "I invited Tim, and there really was only enough for seven."

If he was offended he didn't indicate it but continued to casually munch his carrot until it was gone.

"Do you think you'll ever take Jenny back to Los Angeles?" he asked innocently, changing the subject so abruptly she had no time to consider her answer.

"Never," Aviva answered a bit too quickly, biting her lip against her mistake. He had been very clever, found out just enough about her through the one little word. She shot a glance toward where he stood and saw his eyebrows rise knowingly.

"Then you really are committed to this inn?" He sounded as if he were simply making conversation, but Aviva was wary now. The initial distrust she had felt for him rose to the surface.

"Of course I am," she answered, her mood visibly cooled, "I could never just leave Whaler's Inn to a stranger. I couldn't—wouldn't—leave it to anyone's care but my own. I've worked too hard on it." Suddenly she was lost in her thoughts, going back to the first day she had seen the old house, and it was almost as if Jeremy weren't there. "It's like one of Tim's windows. Some of them he can't bear to part with because he's put too much tender loving care into them. He could never accept mere money for one of those windows. Well, this is my labor of love. I could never give it up. Not for anything...or anyone."

Aviva turned, knowing her last word had been a carefully aimed barb at the man she suddenly remembered stood so near. Her green eyes searched his face for some hint of what was in his mind, but there was nothing there for her to read. Yet her eyes told him everything—about her determination and her loneliness. Which, he wondered, would get the best of her? Knowing Aviva Thompson, he surmised she would have whatever she wanted in the world. If only he could understand what kept her at arm's length.

Softening as she looked into his black eyes, Aviva continued, "Sometimes I find it just a little hard even sharing this place with anyone who has enough money to pay for a room. But you can't pick and choose. It's not like inviting your best friends over for the weekend. But I do love it. The good and bad of it. No, Jenny and I are going to be around here a very long time."

"I think you do believe that, Aviva," was all that Jeremy said.

"I don't just believe it," she answered, raising her chin defiantly, "I know it."

"Maybe, maybe," he mused, crossing his arms over his muscular chest, "but someday you may find that a building just isn't enough. A building can get awfully cold sometimes without someone to share it with."

"I have Jenny," she retorted immediately.

"I don't mean that kind of sharing." Jeremy's feet moved so slowly that she was barely aware he was moving toward her until he stood as close as a person could without touching. Aviva's intake of breath was so quick, so slight, that he didn't even notice. Nor did he notice the almost imperceptible shaking that coursed through her body as he continued to speak. "I mean the kind between a man and a woman. The kind of warmth that can't come from a child. Aviva..." His hand reached up as if to stroke her cheek. That movement shocked her into action and she moved back, away from his disconcerting presence, removing her apron as she did so.

"I'm not sure I want to have this discussion," she said, her voice shaking, her mind confused by her answer. She should have simply told him she didn't want to talk about it, that it was none of his business. Instinctively, though, she knew he was stronger than she and that she cared more about him than she was even willing to admit to herself.

"I have to change for dinner. Perhaps I'll see you later on," Aviva said, turning to flee from him through the kitchen door and up the stairs.

Aviva closed the door to her personal haven with relief. Slowly, she paced back and forth in her room, stopping every now and then to pick up one of her perfume bottles or absentmindedly finger the lace curtains and gaze out over the wild grass to the bluffs above the ocean.

She couldn't deny it any longer. Jeremy Crowley was a danger. Each time she looked at him, spoke to him, each moment longer he was at the inn she realized that her thoughts were of loving him. She wanted it so much, yet it caused such pain.

All her memories warned her not to get involved, to stay clear of a man like him. He could change any minute. Sensitivity could be a learned trait. Perhaps he was really the man who appeared on her doorstep that first night. The man she couldn't stand. Maybe it was just Carmel and the peace of the inn that had transformed him into the gentleman who sat with her night after night.

God, but she wanted him. Wanted him to go, to stay. Wanted him to change so that she would not care for him. She was so confused, undone by her feelings for him.

Finally, glancing at the clock, she decided she had better bathe and dress so that she could be ready to greet her guests for dinner. Aviva knew that she must continue to remind herself that Jeremy Crowley would be gone, out of her life, in a short while. She must not waste her energy trying to solve a problem that didn't exist. In a little while he would be gone, she reminded herself as her fingers reached to unbutton her blouse. A short knock on the door stopped her before even the first one was undone.

He couldn't, wouldn't, have followed me up here, she thought frantically, her hands already beginning to shake in anticipation of what she would find when she opened the door. But crossing the room and flinging the door wide, she was surprised not to find Jeremy but Jenny, who stood, determined and looking peeved, on the red Oriental runner in the center of the hall.

"Hi there, sweet pea!" Aviva's face brightened quickly and considerably as she looked at her daughter. "Did you come for a visit?" In answer to her question Jenny walked, as regally as a three-foot five-year-old could, into the plush, rose-colored room.

"You don't have the fire on, Mommy. You're going to catch cold." Aviva smiled. Two years at that posh nursery school had turned her daughter into a precocious child. Sometimes she thought that Jenny was really a grown-up in disguise.

"You're absolutely right. I'll get it started right now." Jenny had settled herself on the needlepoint footstool by the hearth and watched carefully as her mother attended to the kindling. She didn't speak a word, and Aviva wondered if she had truly neglected the child so much that Jenny might be angry with her.

"Do you want to come in while I take my bath?" Aviva ventured once the fire had caught. Jenny nodded and followed her mother into the gaily papered room. The little girl rushed to the tub.

"I'll get the water. I know how to do it." Her little hands flew about twisting the faucets, adding the bath oil and checking the temperature now and again as Aviva watched. Then Jenny perched herself on the lid of the white wicker hamper and watched her mother undress.

Aviva slipped out of her slacks and shirt and handed the garments to Jenny, who folded them with the exaggerated care that children use. Her mother smiled, amused, as she looked at the crumpled clothes so carefully held in the little lap, knowing that, because of Jenny's "help," she would have to iron them both before putting them back in the armoire.

Slipping into the warm, frothy water, she lay back, considering her silent daughter. It wouldn't be long before Jenny wouldn't want to sit and chat with her as she bathed. But she hoped the little girl would always know that her mother was her best friend. For her daughter, Aviva wanted to be life's costar, never an insignificant part of the chorus.

Jenny, too, was deep in thought, surveying her mother noncommittally until the dark-haired woman had settled into the tub, signaling that they could now have a quiet discussion before dinner. Aviva closed her eyes and listened to the wind whipping about the inn. Then she spoke, her voice deep and throaty, enjoying the bath. "You want to help me wash my back in a minute, sweetheart?"

Opening her eyes in response to the silence that greeted her question, Aviva looked at her daughter, who sat stoically on the white hamper. Her little face was serious and her bottom lip had disappeared under her front teeth as she bit down on the soft skin thoughtfully. Aviva sat up, the lower half of her hair plastered to her back in long ropes. She hated the feeling of wet hair against her skin and gathered the tresses into her right hand holding them away from her neck as she looked questioningly at her daughter.

"Mommy, what was Daddy like?"

So, Aviva thought, *she does remember.*

Laying back into the warm water, Aviva thought for a moment, letting her arms float lifelessly by her sides. How was she going to answer this one? She had known that eventually Jenny would want to hear about what happened to her father, but she had not anticipated that it would be so soon. Jenny was bright and overly curious for her age but she was not old enough to comprehend the fine shadings of her relationship with Sam, Aviva thought.

"Your father was a wonderful man in his own way," she began hesitantly. "He was always happy, always keeping himself busy with one thing or another. Do you remember much of him?"

Jenny shook her head no, and Aviva continued. "Everyone loved your father." Aviva smiled wryly as she answered. Had Jenny been much older Aviva might have explained about Sam's infidelities, but for now she would make it simple. "He was one of those people who brought sunshine into every room... even when it was raining outside...and he loved you best of all." Aviva's voice was lively as she hurried on, beginning to believe that this was truly the Sam she had lived with for so many years. After all, he had been a good man; he had just wanted to live a different life than Aviva.

Deep in her heart she knew he was as disappointed in her as she was in him. She also knew that he had loved her and Jenny more than anything in the world until his dying day. That was the simple truth. Did anything matter other than that? It was a question

Aviva could not answer. She did not want to think about it, fearing that when she did tell herself the truth it might change the wonderful facade she had built for herself and Jenny. The front would change to an actual world in which she would have to deal with sad feelings.

"Yes," Jenny said, her face brightening, "he was just like Jeremy."

Aviva smiled. *From the mouths of babes*... she thought ruefully, knowing that, indeed, the pretty picture she had just painted of Sam did truly sound like the Jeremy they had come to know there at the inn.

"Mommy, don't you ever get bored without Daddy?"

"My goodness, but we are full of questions this evening, aren't we?" Aviva countered, hoping to steer the conversation away from a topic that Jenny really couldn't comprehend.

"Well?" The child was persistent.

"Of course I miss your daddy, but I don't think 'bored' is the word for it." Aviva bit her lip against the little white lie. She didn't really miss Sam. Parts of him, yes, but not the way their life had been in the end, only the way it had been at the beginning. "But I have you and the inn and Mrs. Barber—she's fine company, isn't she?" Aviva had tried to keep her feelings about Gladys Barber to herself because Jenny was so taken with the woman. What was it about children that could melt anyone, even the most unfriendly sorts?

Jenny was silent and thoughtful as she contemplated her pudgy fingers. Aviva could almost hear her mind whirling as she attempted to understand what her mother was saying. For some reason Jenny seemed bursting at the seams with questions she wasn't sure how to ask. It was amusing to watch her struggle so as her little mind tried to form the deep thoughts she was having and to put them into words.

"Well, what about Tim?"

Aviva groaned and slid deeper into the water. "Oh, Jenny, you know that Tim's the best friend we have. Yes, he's included in the list, too."

"What about Jeremy?" she persisted.

"Jeremy is included, too. He's a very nice man but he won't be around like Tim and Mrs. Barber. Remember, he's our guest," Aviva patiently explained.

"I know." Jenny sighed a sigh so heavy that Aviva chuckled. "I just wish he could stay with us all the time, don't you?"

"Well," Aviva said, picking up the bar of soap from the tray, "he is very nice but I'm not sure if I'd want him here all the time."

"Why not?" Jenny parlayed.

"Oh, enough is enough," Aviva cried, good-naturedly exasperated. "I'm not going to tell you why because I don't know myself at this moment, so let's just leave it at that. Besides, he has lots of friends where he lives and I'm sure he misses them. He has a business, too, and it probably keeps him just as busy as the inn keeps us. Would you like it if he said, 'Come and stay with me and never go back to Carmel again'?"

"No," she answered, picking at the hem of her blouse.

"Well, then, don't ask questions like that."

Aviva sat up; the water was now tepid and uncomfortable. "Now, no more talk about people coming and going. Do you want to help me wash my back?"

Jumping down from her perch, Jenny smiled at her mother. "No, thank you. I'll go get dressed now." Still clutching Aviva's clothes in her arms Jenny turned at the door, one more question on her lips.

"No." Aviva laughed before Jenny could even speak, splashing her fleeing, giggling daughter with water. How could she have borne such an inquisitive creature, she thought happily to herself.

Stepping out of the bath, Aviva realized that Jeremy would be leaving in less than two days, and the thought along with Jenny's questioning made her understand just how much she would miss him.

Well, nothing she could do about it. She should listen to herself more often. Jeremy certainly had a life in L.A. and was probably anxious to return to it, despite the relationship that had developed between them. Picking up the soft, warm towel, Aviva began to dry herself and think about all the things that had to be done around the inn.

It hadn't taken her long to dress, but no one would have guessed from the end result. Her costume was overpowering in its simplicity. The chocolate-brown knit pants and tunic skimmed her body. She had a long length of ivory beads around her neck, a matching bangle on her left wrist. The effect was stunning although Aviva would have been hard pressed to believe that had any one of her guests verbalized their appreciation.

By the time she joined her guests for aperitifs, Jenny was already entertaining them with stories of her daily adventures. Aviva, feeling subdued, decided not to interfere, then noticed with amusement that Jenny had worn her Donald Duck slippers under the long dress she had chosen for dinner that evening. Mrs. Barber had brought her knitting down to the main room and was watching the proceedings seemingly with great enjoyment from the corner rocking chair.

At the sound of the bell chimes, Jenny ran from the cozy group to see who had entered.

"It's Tim," she announced on her return, with the untutored nonchalance only a child could conjure up. She had the tall, bearded young man by the hand and left him at her mother's side, then resumed her place on the rug in front of the fireplace.

"I thought it would be Jeremy," she stated before turning back to the young couple who had checked in the day before.

Only Tim and Aviva seemed to have taken any notice of her comment, and Aviva felt Tim tighten in reaction. Neither had noticed Gladys Barber look up to peruse Aviva's face after Jenny's offhand comment. Her needles simply clicked a bit faster as the fire popped.

"I think it's time I checked on dinner. Tim, it will be about ten minutes, if you'd like to have a drink and introduce yourself," Aviva said, heading for the kitchen.

"No, thanks, on the drink." Tim moved away toward a vacant chair handing her a bottle as he went. "Here, this is for dinner."

Aviva took the gift and stopped long enough to allow a smile to grace her lips in thanks. He was so sweet.

Almost immediately Tim's kind and caring face was replaced by the image of Jeremy Crowley, and Aviva shook her head trying to banish it before Tim noticed her strange look. Ashamed of her mental wanderings, Aviva quickly headed for the kitchen.

Sue had things well under control in the kitchen and it was exactly seven-thirty when Aviva called her guests to the dining-room table. Her spirits were revived, all thoughts of Jeremy gone, as she looked about, noting the gleaming silver and crystal, the fresh flowers and the obvious enjoyment of her guests. She was grateful for the few guests she had had that week and realized that the inn was getting off to a fine start and her worry over money was beginning to ebb.

After the usual thanks the table cleared, leaving Tim, Aviva and Gladys to themselves.

"Aviva," Mrs. Barber's curt voice commanded attention. "I have to go into town tomorrow to see my lawyer. I think it would do you good to get out. Why don't you plan on having your girl in all day while we go shopping."

Aviva's mouth dropped. Gladys Barber asking her to go shopping? Worried about her getting out? It was too much to believe. Aviva's first instinct was to decline the offer but something in the old woman's face made her reconsider. *Why not*, she thought. Things couldn't get any worse than they were. Maybe if she went she could figure out exactly where this little bird of a woman was coming from.

"All right," she said, watching carefully for any sign of a complaint that might follow the invitation. "That does sound nice. Jenny and I would love to."

"Nope, we'll just leave the little one here. You need a day all by yourself. Adult company can be very rewarding, you know." The woman stared at Aviva as if to convey some hidden message, but Aviva couldn't figure out what it was for the life of her. Crossing her fingers under the table, she just hoped that this was the beginning of a better relationship with Gladys.

"All right, just the older girls on the town," she said, smiling a genuine smile at Gladys Barber for the first time.

"Good! Now I'm sure you young folks will excuse me," she said as she patted the silver-gray bun on the top of her head, "I'm a bit tired. Think I'll go up to sleep. 'Night." With that she turned and left them alone.

Tim had been rather quiet all evening but Aviva was not too concerned. She had seen him that way before. The mind of an artist was a difficult thing to fathom.

Aviva leaned toward the center of the table and cupped her slim hands behind the flame of each candle as she softly blew them out. She raised the chandelier light just a bit and started clearing the dishes and serving plates away. Returning for the second batch of plates, she could stand it no longer. "Tim." He looked up, his hands still holding the wineglass over which he was hunched. "What's wrong with you tonight? You're so quiet."

"I thought that guy was gone," Tim answered sullenly.

"What..." Aviva almost asked whom he was referring to and then recalled Jenny's unfortunate statement when she had answered the door and found Tim instead of Jeremy.

"Oh, Jeremy," Aviva said.

"So it's Jeremy now." His tone would have sounded demanding but for his natural timidity.

"Yes, it is," Aviva answered firmly. She was not going to have Tim making judgments on any guest at the inn. And especially not Jeremy, she found herself thinking.

"The way he came in here that first night I thought you would have thrown him out the next morning."

"He's been a perfect gentleman since then and we have all come to enjoy his company. If you hadn't been working so hard maybe you would have been around to get to know him."

"Are you sure that's all there is to it?" Tim looked askance at Aviva, and she raised her chin, slightly defiant.

"Not really. I like him very much." There, it was said. Perhaps Tim would abandon his ideas of a relationship now that she had expressed interest in another man. He didn't have to know right that instant that Jeremy would be gone in another day and a half.

"Well, I just can't see it, that's all. And I only say that for your own good, Aviva."

"Tim—" Aviva's soothing voice filled the room "—please believe me when I tell you that everything is fine here. There's no need for you to worry. Now, where is that happy man I was talking to earlier today? I'd much rather have him for company than the one I've got." She had sat down beside him, her hand resting on his shoulder, her voice brightening in an attempt to make up for the hurt she caused him every day by not returning his feelings for her.

Tim looked at her, his eyes baring every emotion in his heart: anger that another man had seemed to take his place, even for a few days, in Aviva's life; love for a woman he would probably never have; exasperation; a desire to protect the family he had come to care for so much. Then, finally, a look of resignation crossed his face and he smiled at her.

"Just you take care, Aviva Thompson," he warned.

"I will, Tim. And thank you," she answered sincerely. Little did he know how apropos his warning was.

By eleven Tim had forgotten any declarations of love he was going to make while they were alone and had lost himself in the description of the three stained-glass windows he had been commissioned to make for one of the movie stars who lived on the Seventeen-Mile Drive in Monterey.

Aviva sat quietly listening to his excited chatter, pleased that he was so consumed by his art rather than by her. The commission could not have come at a better time for her sake.

Neither of them had time to react between the sound of the front door opening and the appearance of a large figure looming in the doorway of the living room. The man stood for a moment, out of the range of the dying firelight. It was only the silver at the temples that registered in Aviva's mind before he spoke.

"Hi." Jeremy's cheery greeting broke the spooky spell of his entrance. Both Aviva and Tim breathed an audible sigh of relief.

Chapter Four

"Jeremy!" Aviva reprimanded. "You scared us half out of our wits!"

"That's not exactly what he scared me out of," Tim agreed, angry with himself that he had been frightened by the sudden appearance of the man but angrier still that Jeremy had appeared at all. Then looking at each other, the two suddenly burst out in nervous laughter as Jeremy moved to join them.

"Next time I'll announce myself by yelling from the doorway. Will that suit you two scaredy-cats?" He smiled at Aviva, then turned to Tim. "Nice to see you, Tim."

The friendly gesture threw the younger man off guard but he automatically raised his hand to shake Jeremy's. Aviva watched as Tim fought his emotions: a flicker of doubt, a moment's reluctance, then the decision to bury his personal hatchet. Tim's lips smiled hesitantly through his beard.

For a moment Jeremy and Tim stood locked in their seemingly friendly stance as if trying to read each other's mind while Aviva watched, praying that the new mood would not change the minute Jeremy sat down. But there was no time for the mood to change, for Jeremy was as antsy as a child at Christmas.

Turning from Tim, he quickly grasped Aviva's hand and spoke as he pulled her up from where she sat. "I can hardly wait until you see the surprise I've got," he babbled as he dragged his willing captive after him toward the door. "Tim, you've got to see this, too. Come on," he called over his shoulder.

"Jeremy, calm down. We haven't seen you all day and then you rush in here like the house is on fire. Where are you taking us?" Aviva's laugh belied her commanding words, and both men knew that she was more than a little intrigued by the promised surprise.

"Come on, Aviva. Now is no time to question me, no time for rational thinking. When you see what I've brought you'll be just as excited as I am." Before Aviva could reply, Jeremy stopped abruptly and she plunged into his back, Tim into hers.

"Whoa," Tim called as they untangled themselves. "Will somebody slow that guy down? Jeremy, didn't you know that your taillights must be in working order in this state?"

Aviva shot a glance behind her as Tim spoke and was met with his open, delighted smile. Sighing in inward relief at the newfound, albeit tenuous truce, Aviva laughed along with the men.

"I'm sorry. I'm just so excited that I'm running in a million directions. But we can't go out unless Jenny is with us. Where is she?" His eyes searched for the little girl and not finding her in the immediate vicinity he took a step toward the stairs. Aviva held out her hand, shivering involuntarily as it met the warm hardness of chest.

"Jeremy, you know good and well she's asleep, and that's how she's going to stay!" Aviva's words left no room for debate and Jeremy was not about to give up the pleasure of her good graces. Once again he took her hand to lead her out into the chill night air, shrugging cheerily as he did so.

"All right, have it your way, but I wouldn't want to be in your shoes tomorrow morning when she finds out that you wouldn't let me wake her up," he teased.

"Jeremy, come on now. What is this surprise that has you so worked up? It's cold out here." Aviva's good-natured command was met with Tim's hearty agreement as he nodded his assent, clasping his arms about his reed-thin body in a vain attempt to keep warm.

"Right over here, folks. Step this way," Jeremy called as he loosed her hand and rushed ahead toward the car. "Gather round. Now, are you ready?"

Aviva and Tim nodded furiously, their breath visible in the night air. "Yes," they cried in unison.

"May I present the newest addition to Whaler's Inn," Jeremy cried with a dramatic flair as he threw open the door of his impeccable Mercedes, the bright white of his teeth shining in the moonlight. For a moment there was complete silence. Jeremy stared at Aviva and Tim; they stared at the dark interior of the car.

"Jeremy," Aviva demanded, her patience now

wearing thin in the chilly evening, "what kind of joke is this?"

"No joke, honest," he said holding up his hands, his smile fading as he turned and looked into the car. "Just a minute, the surprise has decided to go to sleep."

More confused than ever, Tim and Aviva looked at each other, waiting as Jeremy climbed into the back seat of the car, talking, it would seem, to himself. But he had not gone mad as the other two suspected. Instead, he was talking softly to a gangly, sleepy Irish setter pup who now jumped to the ground and stood behind the tall, dark-haired man.

"Ta-da!" Jeremy yelled into the black night, his arms flung wide, his grin bigger and brighter than ever. Aviva's mouth fell open and Tim simply muttered to himself.

"Jeremy!" Aviva said when she finally recovered her voice, "How could you!"

"Oh, Aviva, you can't be angry," he countered immediately, before the full force of her anger could manifest itself. "Why, you need a dog. He'll make a great burglar alarm, he'll keep your feet warm in the winter, and Jenny will love him. I just know she will." Jeremy was breathless from his entreaties and paused for only a moment.

"He is kind of cute, Aviva," Tim jumped in while Jeremy caught his breath, surprising himself by agreeing with Jeremy.

"But I don't know a thing about dogs, he'll shed all over everything, and—" Before she could list all of her objections the red-haired dog was on her, snuggling about her legs. Looking down, Aviva tried desperately to retain her stern expression as she spoke once again. "And..." Where were all those logical thoughts she had just been thinking? "And, well, we better get this creature inside before it freezes to death."

Unable to resist the furry body that already seemed as if he belonged with her, Aviva bent down, smiling, and scooped up the pup. Turning on her heel, she made her way into the house, followed closely by the two men who were exchanging knowing looks. But by the time Tim and Jeremy reached the foyer, Aviva was already halfway to the kitchen, calling over her shoulder as she went.

"All right, you two. If we're going to keep him we'll have to get him settled. Jeremy, you come in here and find a water dish. Tim, we'll need a blanket from the linen closet." Aviva bustled about chattering away to the dog, Tim and Jeremy in one long, rambling sentence. Finally, the dog was settled and asleep, dozing deeply as puppies do. Quietly, the threesome left the kitchen after spreading the evening paper over the spotless floor.

"Now, how about a nightcap?" Aviva addressed the two men, her hand swishing a stray strand of hair from her eyes as she smiled at them. "After all that excitement I sure could use one. If nothing else, I need it to calm my nerves. I can already hear Jenny's screams of delight when she sees our latest addition." Aviva raised her eyes toward heaven as if her suffering were beyond compare.

"No, thanks," Tim volunteered, feeling suddenly

out of place in the now-quiet house. "I think I'd better get going. Jeremy, nice to see you," the young man ended somewhat self-consciously.

"Thanks," Jeremy's answer was sincere, and some unspoken message seemed to have passed between the two men as they once again shook hands.

"I'll take you up on that drink," Jeremy said as soon as they were alone together.

"All right," Aviva answered, her heart quickening as she looked into his eyes. "Why don't you go ahead and pour me a very small bit of brandy. I'm going to check on our newest boarder just once more."

"That's what I like," Jeremy called after her, "a woman with a heart of steel."

"Enough!" Aviva waved her hand behind her head as she went, dismissing Jeremy with the small gesture. Quickly she peeked into the kitchen, using the time to control her breathing and calm herself before she would once again look into his eyes.

The puppy still slept, curled into a little ball, so that it was hard to tell where the tail began and the nose ended. Smiling to herself as she looked at the helpless little ball of bone and hair, Aviva realized just how special Jeremy was.

The dog was not the most expensive gift Aviva had ever received, but it was the most touching. The puppy was helpless, in need of love, and Jeremy had brought it to her. Softly she shut the door, reflecting on the man's spontaneous gift that had touched her so, and went to take her place by the dying fire with Jeremy.

Their conversation was light while they watched the

embers dwindle and fade. Jeremy was sure that Aviva was pleased with his gift and delighted in recounting the story of how he had come upon the pup. It seemed that, while walking on one of the side streets of Carmel, he had come upon a makeshift stand manned by a little boy. Believing that it was lemonade the kid was selling Jeremy stopped to order a glass. Instead, the boy offered Jeremy one of a litter of puppies.

Declining the offer, Jeremy had gone on his way to complete his business. It wasn't until much later, after dinner, that he once again found his way to the house, determined to take a puppy home for Jenny. The boys' father had tried to pawn off two of the little dogs but Jeremy had stood firm and only accepted one—a fact that he felt should have gained him a bit of Aviva's respect. Finally, she relented and dropped the guise of anger she had tried so hard to sustain.

"Jeremy," she said when he had finished his story for the second time, "I really think you're spoiling Jenny, but I'm sure we'll both love the puppy. And you're right. It never hurts to have a watchdog around the place, though I doubt we would ever have any problems here. Actually, he'll give this old inn a real homey feeling."

"I'm glad you like him. I'd hoped you would. It gives me hope that you might come to like another stray dog that's been hanging around here for the past few days." He chuckled, trying to make light of the statement, but the chuckle died along with the fire and they found themselves alone in the big, silent room, both suddenly shy, almost afraid to break the

quiet: she for fear of what he might say, he for fear of
how she might react.

"I'll be leaving tomorrow night," Jeremy hesitantly
broke the silence. He waited for a response, although
the statement really needed none.

"I know," she acknowledged, a tremulous sigh escaping her lips before she continued. "We'll miss
you."

There, it had been said. Aviva felt almost relieved
that she had finally admitted there was something
more than a proprietor/boarder relationship between
her and Jeremy. He must have known after all these
days, though, that she felt more than a passing friendship toward him. To her dismay, however, he did not
accept the statement on face value.

"We?" he queried, gently probing for the words he
wanted to—must—hear.

"Of course, all of us. Gladys and Jenny and…and
me. Jeremy, I will miss you." The last words were
almost a stifled cry, and Aviva hung her head to hide
her embarrassment.

"And I you, Aviva. More than you can ever believe."

So simple, she thought as she listened to the words.
Said any other way, with any other inflection it could
have been a friendly statement, warm or sarcastic. But
there was no mistaking Jeremy's meaning. There was
caring, deep and warm, in his tone and there was…
there was love. It was a simple sentiment, straightforward and true.

Aviva felt her heart move into her throat, a shiver
run through her body. How easy it would have been

for her to give up and go to him, thank him for feeling the way he did; but Aviva didn't move, didn't know how to answer him, thank him, take him. But she didn't have to worry, for he continued to speak, surprising her more with each word he uttered.

"Aviva, would you come with me to Los Angeles? Let's see what can come of this." His voice gained confidence with every moment that passed and she didn't stop him. "Or if you can't leave now, come in a few days, a few weeks. I just know there is more to this than a beautiful meeting that will never be forgotten. You can't deny it, either. You've felt it—the electricity, the emotions that pass between us each night we sit here in the firelight. Aviva, please come to my home. Please."

"Jeremy." Her voice sounded small and unsure, that in itself an acknowledgment of the truth he spoke. She could deny him verbally, she could simply walk away from him as she had done that very afternoon, but in her heart she would always know he was right. There was something very special between them. Something beautiful and wonderful that could never go any further than the room they now sat in. Must not go any further and would not if she could help it. But could she? Did she have the strength to deny what he was saying, to escape while there was still time?

"I couldn't. There is no one here to run the inn, watch Jenny, and now there's that dog…" Her words trailed off sadly, in no way convincing the man across from her that those were her reasons for denying his request.

Jeremy rose and moved toward her. Her body heat increased as he moved a petit-point footstool to settle himself at her feet. "Aviva, tell me the real reason. I deserve at least that. Tell me why you are so afraid of me. Tell me about you. Why will you only let me in so far? What you have shown me of yourself is so beautiful—show me the rest." His black eyes searched her face as if that action alone could force her to speak the truth.

Aviva shook her head, lowering her eyes, feeling a lump rise to her throat. It had been so long since she had cried. She didn't want to start now for fear that if the tears flowed they might never be dammed.

Jeremy's voice was strained as he gently urged her on, and Aviva detected a note of pleading. His eyes bore into her, begging her to lose herself in him, telling her that nothing she could say would drive him away.

Seeing those eyes clearly now that she sat so close to him, smelling his scent, feeling the strong hands that reached out to hold hers, Aviva sighed a trembling sigh and began to speak.

It was exactly one hour later when she finished. All the years had fallen away as she spoke and Aviva was once again a woman torn by love and dismay as she relived her life. She was a little girl envying the other children at school who would bring two parents rather than one to see the teachers. She was a frightened married woman who was so scared of loving, afraid to admit that men like her husband attracted her, that she had almost forgotten how to love.

They sat quietly across from each other after she

had completed her tale. Their eyes locked, both searching for a sign. Aviva had almost stopped breathing. She felt as if her soul had been cleansed, as if she could now escape the confining emotional cocoon that she had spun so tightly for herself.

It had almost been as if she were speaking to herself: trying to convince the passionate, dormant Aviva that the life she had lived was gone forever. She was drained by her monologue. Now there was no resistance as Jeremy slowly came toward her. He approached as a man, not a guest who had spent friendly evenings chatting in front of the fire with the proprietor.

She felt the pressure of his hands and watched as he bent his head, touching his lips to her fingertips. Aviva thought she felt a tear fall but dismissed the idea as she sat, rigid, looking at the handsome man at her feet. Her heart reached out to him, no longer denying her feelings, but her body could not relax, still held in the grip of her tale.

Gently turning her palms up to meet his lips, he continued to kiss her hands softly, gently, as one might kiss a child frightened in the night by some terrible dream. Still holding her hands in his, he rose slowly, so that she, too, stood up and now found herself a hairbreadth from him. Her eyes did not move to his face but simply considered the intricate pattern of his sweater as his lips began to explore her face, roaming over her smooth brow, nestling in her scented hair.

"My poor darling," he whispered, "my poor, lovely woman. Don't be afraid to love again. Love me now." His arms cradled her body and they moved together, softly rocking, melding in step to unheard music. "I won't hurt you. I would never hurt you."

Aviva closed her eyes, grateful for his warmth, succumbing to his mesmerizing chant of comfort. No longer willing or able to fight against her feelings, she abandoned herself to him, and as his arm slid around her shoulders to lead her up the stairs, she did not protest but nuzzled deeper against his body. He seemed to hesitate for a moment at the top of the stairs, then turned resolutely toward his room.

For the first time, Aviva moved her head, looking up into his face. Smiling softly, her hand reached up to touch the tanned skin and trace the deep lines etched on the side of his eyes, the square jaw softened by his look of longing.

Tonight she would surrender; tomorrow she might have to pay the price. As if he understood her resolution he tightened his grip on her shoulder, trying desperately to reassure her.

Neither spoke a word as they stood before the four-poster. Aviva watched his every move now, the fluid grace as he removed first his coat, then his sweater, revealing his smooth back and powerful arms. In a moment he was facing her, his fingers slowly untying the three bows that fastened her tunic.

The velvety fabric fell open and his hands slipped between the folds, caressing her body, his fingers running like so many falling leaves down the curve of her waist, exploring the soft skin of her stomach hidden just beneath the elastic band of her evening pants.

Aviva shivered as he raised her bra, capturing first

one breast then the other. His hands played momentarily across the soft mounds, tracing leisurely circles on the farthest reaches before capturing her taut nipples between two gentle fingers. Sweetly kissing the fawn-colored orbs, his lips covered first one then the other, nipping and teasing.

Aviva stifled a groan of pleasure. Her head thrown back, she offered her heaving bosom to him, seeking the pleasure only he could give her now, the love she needed from him.

Her hands reached out, cupping his tight buttocks with her hungry fingers, then moved up, rejoicing in the life she found in him. Her fingers traced, unseeing, the outline of the muscles moving and twisting beneath his taut skin as they moved toward the bed. Slowly he lowered her, and the old bed creaked. She moved slightly as he slipped off the tunic and unhooked her bra, releasing her from the confining garment. Aviva could feel him gently move her legs. Closing her eyes, she felt the cool air nip her as he removed the last bit of her clothing. She was lost in a whirlpool of desire. Phantasmic images of color rotated behind her fluttering lids.

Then, as if he were an extension of her dream, he was beside her. Gentle but insistent, his hands and mouth roamed over her body. She reached out for him, desperately trying to touch every inch of his masculine form, but he would not let her. His intimate reprimands spoke more clearly than any words. Tonight, all the pleasure was for her.

But as she felt his warmth and the room filled with the musky scent of love, she could no longer simply accept the wondrous gift he offered her. Desperately she moved into him, her hips pulsating, begging him to enter her, and with an urgency to match hers they met, exploding together in a tempest that tore through their very souls.

Satisfied, they slept, nuzzled in each other's arms, content to express their happiness wordlessly until the gray light of morning.

"Good morning." Jeremy's deep voice floated toward her the moment her eyes opened.

"Hi." Aviva looked at the well-dressed man sitting before the newly lit fire. Quickly her eyes moved to the window, noting the fog-softened sunlight. She moved and raised herself on one elbow, careful to keep the quilt up around her shoulders.

"How long have you been up?" She searched her mind for something to say, wishing he would leave and let her get dressed. Her embarrassment both amused and confused her. It was not as if she had never slept with a man before. Yet with Jeremy sitting there, she felt as virginal as a sixteen-year-old caught with her first love.

"Oh, about all night. You are so beautiful when you're asleep I don't know how I could have closed my eyes at all." He was not going to give her any privacy and she had to get back to her room before Jenny woke up and the rest of the house stirred.

"I really should be getting back to my room." Her embarrassment was now painfully evident and her cheeks burned though her lips smiled at him warmly. Jeremy rose from the chair and settled himself on the bed beside her, gently pushing her back into the pillows. She watched him warily. Was he going to try to make love to her again? But that was not his intention and she was almost disappointed when he spoke.

"You can rest for just a minute while we talk. Then I'll let you get dressed while I put on the coffee." Jeremy's eyes crinkled as he smiled down at her, amused by the look on her face.

"So you thought I would attempt to ravish you again so early in the morning? Well, I'll have to disappoint you. Not because I don't want to, you understand. I just don't want to push my luck." His good humor was catching, and Aviva relaxed in the warm bed. Before she had time to make a sound he continued. "Now, last night..."

She held her breath. Aviva felt wonderful. Not only physically satisfied but content in the company of this man. But once again she was on her guard. This introduction to his speech sounded ominous.

"Aviva, I have never enjoyed being with a woman so much in my entire life. And, well, there have been a few."

So, this was it. Love 'em and leave 'em. She steeled herself for what was to come. How could she have been so stupid as to think that he was different. Again, he was going to disappoint her. His next words banished any misgivings she had had.

"But I have never *loved* being with a woman... until last night." His face was serious, watching hers for encouragement. Finding only questions, he went on.

"I think I love you. I have thought it from the moment I met you. If you're not ready for that now, I'll wait. I'll wait for as long as it takes. I could probably use a little time to figure this out myself, anyway." She started to speak, but his fingers moved and covered her lips, the scent of his after-shave still fresh.

Aviva was grateful for the gesture. Had he not restrained her she was not sure what she would have said. Her heart wanted to cry out to him, tell him she loved him, too. But her mind rationalized. How could it be, their love for each other? They came from the same world but now lived in two different ones. No, she could not go back with him. But he didn't want to hear that now. Nor did she wish to say the words that would send him away.

"Don't say a word," he urged her, driving away all the thoughts she was having. "Just lie there for a few minutes, then go get that little minx down the hall and we'll all have breakfast. But please think about the offer. We should have every chance. Life could be so wonderful, Aviva, if you just give it a little help."

She enjoyed the sound of the bed creaking as he rose to go. By the door he stopped as if he'd forgotten something. "I snuck into your room a few hours ago. That hideous terry robe of yours is in the bathroom." With that and a smile he was gone, leaving Aviva relieved that he had not asked her for an immediate answer to his proposal.

Alone now, Aviva slipped into the robe and out of his room, quietly making her way to her own, where she quickly showered and dressed. Fifteen minutes later she was ready to join him in the kitchen. Her alacrity left no room for introspection. After a final brush to her hair, Aviva looked into Jenny's room.

The little girl was not there but her whereabouts was evident the moment Aviva stepped out into the hall. There she was greeted by Jenny's squeals of laughter wafting up from the foyer and Jeremy's call of "Here, boy."

The dog! Aviva said to herself, *I've forgotten about the dog!* Quickly she danced down the stairs just in time to see the puppy slide across the newly waxed floor.

"All right, you two." Aviva stopped at the landing, enjoying the sight before her but knowing that some semblance of order had to be restored. "The dog belongs in the kitchen. Has he been taken out this morning or do we have a mess in there?"

"The mess was there, of course, but it is all cleaned, madam," Jeremy answered, coming to mock attention. For the first time she noted the long white apron he wore over his clothing, but before she could comment he offered a salute. "And your breakfast is almost on the table."

"Okay. At least things are under control. Now scoot, both of you. I mean all three of you," she commanded, fighting to keep her giggles from escaping.

Jeremy scooped up the dog and headed toward the kitchen. Jenny, grabbing Aviva's hand, followed close behind, chattering as they followed.

"Can I name the puppy, Mommy?" she queried as they entered the kitchen.

"Of course you can," she answered, crossing over to disentangle the creature from Jeremy's legs while he tried to fry the bacon. "What shall it be?" she asked, settling herself on the kitchen chair as she held the pup on her lap while Jenny petted it enthusiastically.

"Um, how about Happy?" the little girl asked seriously, bobbing back and forth in front of the dog, who kept playfully nipping the air, yapping at the hands that tried to pet it.

"Or how about Red?" Aviva countered as Jenny nodded her head in agreement.

"Come on, you two, let's get a little creative. What about Scarlet or Cardinal or Cherry?" Jeremy added his thoughts as he turned the bacon for the last time.

"Cherry, Cherry." Jenny giggled.

"Cherry it is, then," Aviva agreed and set the little dog down. "Now, Jenny, I want you to take him out back and make sure he goes to the bathroom before you bring him in. Then, we'll try to find something to feed him until I get to the store for some puppy food."

"Okay, Mommy." With that the two smallest members of the household happily went through the back door. Aviva rose and moved toward Jeremy, who was efficiently removing the bacon from the pan and draining it on a stack of paper towels.

"Can I help?" she asked, her eyes roaming over the muscular back that had so recently been hers to explore. A shiver ran through her, and she restrained herself from reaching out and touching his shoulders, which were now covered with a light blue cashmere sweater.

"Not with the bacon. Breakfast is under control," he answered before turning around to face her, a greasy fork in his hand, "but the chef could use some encouragement of another kind." His black eyes danced playfully as he watched her. Without thinking, driven simply by the desire to feel him once again, Aviva moved in to him, her lips meeting his with an intensity that surprised her. For an instant she allowed herself to lean against him, then quickly retreated back to her chair.

"Well," he teased, "that's a start, but if we're going to keep this up I'll expect a longer bout of encouragement than that."

Aviva blushed both with pleasure at the feel of him and concern that perhaps she was leading him on, allowing him to hope for more than was possible. Hearing Jenny's voice grow louder, though, she decided that the moment was not right for the serious discussion she knew they must have.

As Jenny and the dog reentered the kitchen, Aviva laid down the ground rules for Cherry's new life and Jenny nodded seriously as if every word were law. Aviva knew it would only be a matter of time before she herself would be responsible for the care and feeding of Cherry and the dog would be lounging in front of the fireplace in the living room instead of in the kitchen where he belonged. But she knew she would really not object. She was as taken with the dog as Jenny was. As long as he stayed in the kitchen until he was housebroken, she would be happy.

"All right, everybody, soup's on." Jeremy interrupted the lecture as he set plates of steaming eggs, bacon and muffins on the table and shooed Jenny to her seat.

"Jeremy," Jenny said in the only moment she took her eyes off the dog, "can you play with me and Cherry all day?"

"Jenny," Aviva's stern voice caused the two to look her way. "I think Jeremy's got plenty to do without playing with you and that dog all day long." She smiled then, realizing that her words had been far too harsh to fit the occasion. "I mean..." Self-consciously, she tried to rectify her statement, but Jenny really was getting out of hand and Jeremy was spoiling her dreadfully.

"It's all right, Aviva." Jeremy reached out and placed a hand on her arm, somehow knowing that the events of the last few days had finally caught up with her. "I think I can find some time this morning to start Cherry's training."

"Thank you," she answered, smiling weakly at him, then turning to Jenny. "As long as he says it's all right, I guess I can't object."

Jenny smiled, but ate the rest of her breakfast in silence. As soon as the last plate had been cleaned, the last muffin eaten, Aviva rose from her chair.

"You three better get started if you're going to have that dog trained today," she said, her good humor returning. "I'll do the dishes, since Jeremy was kind enough to cook. Now out, both of you, and leave me alone."

They were both out the door in a second, dragging Cherry along with them on a leash made of string. Aviva smiled as she watched them go. The puppy looked so awkward, with its long legs and snout. But Aviva knew only too well that it would grow into a big dog with a big appetite, and her amusement dimmed in the light of the thought.

Contentedly she set about cleaning the kitchen, her mind wandering away from the scene in the backyard and back to the events of the night before.

She had forgotten what it was like to be pleased by a man in bed. There were certain things she had not enjoyed leaving behind when she closed herself off from her old world. Had she stayed in Los Angeles she probably would have had many lovers—men were so plentiful and so willing there. Jeremy had been wonderful. A kind, considerate and passionate lover. His timing was perfect, his declaration of love not unwelcome and his warmth cherished.

But his invitation to accompany him to Los Angeles was impossible. The memories, the hurt, the dislike for the place were still too fresh in her mind. She didn't want to know him away from the inn. She didn't want to find out that he could be any different than he had been for the past four days. That would be an awakening she could not face.

Glancing through the window as she plunged her hands into the hot, soapy water, Aviva watched him playing with her daughter and repeated over and over to herself that it was impossible even to consider his suggestion. She would not, could not, go with him. She knew that it would be the beginning of the end of everything she had worked for, every vow she had made to herself. Then she saw Jenny running toward the house as Jeremy followed with the dog. Only moments later Jenny burst through the door, happier than Aviva had ever seen her.

"Mommy, Jeremy's going to take us to Shadowbrook, but only if you say okay." He had followed her in and stood looking at Aviva. Shrugging his shoulders as if to deny all complicity in the plan, Jeremy looked like a schoolboy.

"Well, I don't know." Aviva was hesitant. She had asked Sue to watch the inn the following day and she didn't want to impose on the girl on such short notice. Especially now that Cherry had joined the household.

"Good morning all," Mrs. Barber's greeting cut short Aviva's train of thought. "Mr. Crowley, nice to see you looking so domestic." She acknowledged the apron he still wore but didn't give him a chance to speak. "And what have we here?" Gladys bent to take the puppy in her arms.

"That's Cherry," Jenny volunteered enthusiastically. "Jeremy brought him and now he's going to take us to Shadowbrook for lunch. They have a tram and everything. But Mommy hasn't said we can go yet." Jenny was breathless and Aviva stepped in while her daughter was momentarily silent.

"I don't know, sweetheart. I promised to take Gladys into town. Sue is going to be here all day and..." Aviva so wanted to go. Jeremy would be leaving so soon and she had to give him an answer one way or another. Maybe it would be easier to make a decision if she spent this time with him. It was Gladys Barber who solved her dilemma for her, and Aviva found herself blessing the old woman for what she would have considered interference only days before.

"Don't want to hear another word about it, Miss. I

can go see that old lawyer anytime. You and Jenny and this delightful boy have my permission to take the whole day off. I'll watch the inn and this little darling. I grew up around dogs. Know how to handle them. That is, if you trust me," she finished crustily, her obvious entrancement with the dog belying her tone.

"Of course I do. It's just that..." Aviva knew it was an imposition, but she wasn't going to look a gift horse in the mouth. After all, Gladys certainly did take to the dog and she was probably happy to be so needed. This was a side of Gladys she never knew existed and she found that she liked it. The woman had a soft spot after all.

"Oh, honestly, this is a conspiracy." Aviva feigned frustration, trying not to smile, "Okay, we'll go, but I have a few things to do around here before we start. Let's say ten o'clock?" She raised her eyebrows, questioning Jeremy. Then turning to Gladys Barber, she smiled sincerely, trying to find the words to thank her but only finding something in the old woman's eyes that told her she already knew how important the outing was.

"Good," Gladys answered for him, impatient as usual, "now that that's settled have you got breakfast ready, Jeremy?"

"Coming right up. But I'm afraid Aviva will have to do the dishes twice," he answered as he prepared to tackle the stove again. Before long he set a plate in front of her and once again they gathered about the table while Aviva puttered around the kitchen.

Jeremy and Jenny amused the two women with their happy banter as Gladys ate her breakfast. Jeremy had proven to be a most worthy cook, and Aviva joked that she should hire him full-time, blushing when he suggested that it could be arranged. The jocular mood was only disturbed when Tim appeared, saying he had to fix the window on the widow's walk. His grim appearance surprised Aviva and put a damper on the hilarity around the table. For a moment it was hard to recapture the mood, especially after he refused to sit down to breakfast.

While Gladys and Jeremy and Jenny went about their business, Aviva stole a few moments from her chores and went in search of Tim. Climbing the steep stairs to the steeple where he was working, she stepped out onto the narrow balcony that overlooked the ocean.

Aviva would have liked to have known the person who dubbed the narrow little balcony a widow's walk. She could imagine a woman, dressed all in black, skirts blowing about her ankles, staring for hours on end out to sea, praying for a glimpse of the wooden ship that would bring her man home from his adventures. How horrible it must have been those many years ago when all a woman could do was sit and wait. She sighed gratefully, knowing that her destiny was her own, no matter what decisions she made. Tim was angrily removing caulking from one of the leaded panes when she came upon him.

"Be careful. If you break the glass you'll hate yourself." Tim didn't answer but sullenly continued with his work. Looking at him, she realized just how different their worlds were. Jeremy would never act like this. Tim was simply a boy compared to the worldly man inside. But he was a boy who could offer her undying loyalty and love if she decided that was what she needed.

Then again, she was probably better off alone. Looking out to the gray sea, she decided not to think about all the "ifs" in her life. But Tim was as close to family as Aviva had in Carmel and she couldn't leave him here alone without getting some explanation of his strange behavior. He had seemed to accept, even be happy about, the situation at the inn the night before.

His silence was worrisome, and Aviva tried once again to cajole Tim into a conversation. "You know the old adage: You break it, you buy it," she teased.

"You forget—I already have," Tim shot back sullenly. Aviva was taken aback by the reference to his investment in the window but had no time to think about it before he spoke again. "God, Aviva, I'm sorry. I just can't believe how things change from day to day. First, Jeremy comes and changes things around here and this morning I got a call from Monterey. That guy doesn't want me to do the windows now."

"Oh, Tim, I'm sorry," Aviva said sincerely. "What happened?"

"He said he got some big-name artist to do it. I guess he cares more about a name than the work." Tim chipped harder at the caulking, then his shoulders fell in defeat and he let his hands slip to his sides as he finally looked at her. "Listen, don't mind me. I guess this just isn't my month."

"Look," Aviva said, trying to ease his disappointment a little, "there are just some people who care more about appearances than others. Don't let it get to you. They aren't important. Really, they're not," she insisted.

"I guess you should know." Tim smiled back weakly.

How right he was, Aviva thought ruefully. Thank goodness all that was behind her now. No more plastic people, no more hustle and bustle of reaching for the stars. Poor Tim, what a rude awakening for him. Well, he had to learn sometime. It was amazing that he hadn't experienced such snobbishness until now.

"I also know that disappointments have a way of fading. Some big ones take a long time but others—they're gone almost in an instant. You just have to decide how long you're going to let it get to you." Tim simply nodded, then resumed his work.

"Now, don't work too long up here. Jenny and I are going to be out today so Gladys will be watching the house."

"Okay," Tim answered, once more absorbed in his work and his thoughts. He didn't look up as Aviva passed quickly through the small door, thankful that she didn't have to explain her unusual absence. All he needed now was to be reminded of Jeremy. She could hear his angry scraping grow fainter as she picked her way carefully down the stairs. She was thoughtful as she descended to the lower level, and the heavy rugs muffled her steps as she moved through the entry and back toward the kitchen.

She could hear Jeremy, Jenny and Gladys out in the yard with the dog, and the sound of the happy voices warmed her heart as no other could. *Poor Tim,* she thought, *I hope he will be happy.* But instantly she knew he would. Tim never let anything get him down long. It wouldn't be more than a few hours and he would be back at his shop absorbed in one project or another.

Checking her watch, Aviva noted that it was almost time to leave for Shadowbrook. Quickly she moved about the house straightening and dusting, moving pictures and emptying trash cans. Finally she ran upstairs to her own room to comb her hair and freshen up just a bit. She was actually looking forward to the day away more than she could say when she heard a light tap on her door. Before she could open it Jeremy slipped in, closing the door behind him. Aviva grinned as he approached her.

"Hi," she whispered. "What are you doing up here?"

"I just couldn't bear to be away from you very long," he whispered back as he approached her, took her in his arms and kissed her. "Why are we whispering?" he said after his lips left hers.

"I don't know. It just seems so illicit, you being in my room and all in broad daylight," she answered, her voice still lowered, her blush charming. Aviva felt as if her boyfriend had eluded her parents in order to see what her room looked like so he could dream about it during geometry class.

"You have a strange sense of illicit," Jeremy teased back, "after last night, that is."

"Jeremy—" Aviva raised her fists in playful protest and lightly beat his chest "—that was different."

"Why? Because it was dark?"

"Oh, but you're insufferable," Aviva said, giggling all the while.

"I know. So why don't you tell me you'll come with me tonight and I won't bother you anymore."

"Not at all?" Aviva flirted.

"Well, maybe just a little." Once again his lips met hers, and Aviva leaned close for an instant, enjoying the scent of him, the cradle his arms made around the small of her back. Then, pushing him away, she showed him to the door.

"I said I'd think about it. Now out, before Jenny or Gladys comes up here." A wave of her hand ushered him out the door and he left, a caricature of despondency. But before she could close the door behind him, he poked his head through once more, stole a kiss and was gone with a warning to hurry because he couldn't control Jenny much longer.

Smiling to herself, Aviva moved around the room as if in a dream, picking up her coat and purse, then finally leaving the room to join her anxious lover and excited daughter.

Jenny was thrilled with the outing, and Aviva was grateful for his patient attentiveness toward her daughter, realizing that people without children sometimes found them overly tiring. But, Jeremy seemed to thrive on the attention the little girl paid him. Aviva was constantly amazed at the new dimension he had brought to both their lives.

Lunch was not only filling but charming. The restaurant had been built low on the side of a mountain, almost hidden from view. Customers were taken to the door by a little tram that only held six people. The ride was short but from the way Jenny reacted one would have thought she had just stepped into a gondola headed up the Alps.

Inside there were nooks and crannies that held chintz-covered tables with fresh flowers. There was color everywhere as the light came through the floor-to-ceiling stained-glass windows. For a minute Aviva was reminded of Tim slaving away back at the inn but she quickly dismissed the thought from her mind.

Today she was determined to enjoy herself. But even as she did, she could not put the question of Jeremy's suggestion out of her mind. How was she going to answer him?

After lunch, they stopped at the small gift store and Jeremy bought Jenny a mug emblazoned with the name Shadowbrook. Finally it was time to leave, and Aviva was sorry to see the day end so quickly. Jenny was asleep almost before Jeremy and Aviva settled themselves in the front seat of the car, and as they drove down the tree-lined road there was the quiet of contentment all about them.

Finally Jeremy broke the silence. "Aviva, I want to know now. Are you going with me tonight?"

Roused from her deep thoughts Aviva turned her head, studying his profile for what seemed like eons. Her heart flew out to him. There was no denying it. She loved this man who seemed to care so much for her as a person, who doted on her daughter, who fulfilled her as a woman. But go with him? Back to L.A.? No. She knew she couldn't do that. She had loved before to no avail. She had been dragged into a life-style she had not chosen and hadn't wanted. And then her responsibility had been only to her daughter. Now it was to Jenny and a business, not to mention the friends she had made in Carmel.

"Jeremy, I can't," she said as she watched his jaw tighten slightly. Aviva knew she should say more, touch him, let him know that she did care deeply, but the words simply would not come.

"Oh, Aviva," he said, sighing, "why not?"

"You know why not. Too many memories and..." She stopped, not knowing how to continue for an instant. Then, gathering her courage, she plunged into her next sentence. "Perhaps my reasons sound silly to you—removed from reality. But for me, this is reality. I have things to do here and, truthfully, I don't think I want to know you back there."

Suddenly the car swerved and Jeremy pulled to a stop on the soft shoulder of the road. Yanking on the hand brake he swiveled in his seat and looked at her. Quietly, so as not to disturb Jenny, he took Aviva by the shoulders and stared deep into her green eyes, whispering urgently. "Aviva, what makes you so certain that I would be different? Los Angeles, Carmel, Timbuktu, I am the same man, you the same woman. Nothing would have to change. Believe me!"

"Jeremy, please." Aviva's voice was pleading now. Her fingertips rose to his lips, hoping to silence him with her slight gesture. How could she hope he would understand when she herself wasn't sure that her reasons were valid?

"All right, all right," he acquiesced. Deflated but not defeated, he took her fingertips and kissed them gently. "But don't think it's going to stop here. We've started something that has to be played out. I can't turn my feelings off and on, and I'll wager you can't, either."

Seeing the tears welling up in her eyes, the eyes he loved so much, Jeremy stopped speaking and simply took her in his arms, allowing her head to rest on his shoulder before he gently pushed her away and moved the car out onto the road.

Aviva settled back into her seat and they drove on in silence once again. Deep in her heart there was a part of her that openly wept over what she was sure must be the loss of Jeremy Crowley.

Chapter Five

Jeremy carried Jenny gently into the house. The little girl had not stirred during the trip home, and now she lay deep in sleep on the settee under the bay window in the living room. As Aviva covered her with the pearl-colored afghan Mrs. Barber had finished the night before, Jeremy disappeared upstairs to pack.

Aviva stood for a moment, her eyes turned toward the living-room door contemplating Jeremy's refusal to accept her word that she would never return with him to Los Angeles. His promise that he would not let their relationship rest unnerved her. If only she could believe him, know once and for all that there was a chance for a normal, healthy life with him for both her and Jenny.

There was no doubt in her mind that Jeremy truly believed he could not do without her once he returned to Los Angeles. If she had learned anything about him, it was that he was a man of honesty and sincerity. But Aviva knew only too well how people changed when circumstances dictated their movements—how responsibility to a family could seem dull and boring next to the lure of parties, contacts, business deals and sheer "bought and paid for" beauty.

Oh, Jeremy, she thought wistfully, *you have certainly convinced yourself that it could work. How I wish you could convince me.*

The thought was immediately replaced by another. Was she being fair to the man upstairs? Perhaps once he was gone the old adage "out of sight, out of mind" would apply to her, too. Wouldn't the inn and Jenny once again command all her time, so that Jeremy Crowley would simply fade into the region of warm memories and cherished, captured moments?

Shaking her head, Aviva realized that the questions could not be answered there in the gathering dusk of the living room while he was still about. Maybe she would never dare even to contemplate them again once he was gone, once she could not look into his deep, dark eyes or feel the strength of his body next to hers. In a vain attempt to clear her head, Aviva sighed a deep, gut-wrenching sound and moved silently out of the room.

"Well, you're finally back. Thought you'd decided to make a night of it, too, when it got past three...." Mrs. Barber did not look up for more than an instant when Aviva entered the kitchen. Her face was flushed a becoming pink from the steam rising about her. Her usually impeccable bun was askew and a few strands of soft silver hair had escaped, curling coquettishly about her thin face. She had never looked happier. Aviva wondered if she had ever treated her husband with the same curtness when all the while she was having the time of her life doing little chores for him.

Aviva was beginning to think that Gladys's outward disdain for people was no more than a sham, and the thought made her somehow more tolerant of the woman.

Tim sat, his long legs dangling, on the far corner of the tiled counter munching happily on a piece of celery, his mustache glistening with the foam from a beer he had just put down.

"We might as well have stayed out all night. It looks like you two really have things under control here," Aviva said brightly, though Jeremy's imminent departure still weighed heavily on her mind. The sight of these two people, so obviously content with what life had to offer in Carmel, warmed her heart. *This is how I want to be always,* Aviva reminded herself. Safe and warm and surrounded by people who wanted to be where she was.

"What are you cooking for dinner?" She leaned over the steaming Dutch oven, grabbing a carrot that lay on the cutting board. Like lightning, Mrs. Barber's birdlike hand shot out and slapped her wrist gently.

"None of that. Tim's been eating enough for an army, and there won't be anything left in the pot if you start."

"All right. But what are you making? It smells delicious!" Aviva's personal confusion dissipated as the safety of the kitchen and its occupants engulfed her.

"Just an old-fashioned pot roast and vegetables. Since everyone is out tonight except for family, I figured we didn't have to impress anyone with that fancy cooking you're always doing." Gladys sniffed.

Neither of them noticed Aviva's surprised smile.

She never would have guessed that Mrs. Barber considered herself family. Far from upsetting Aviva, the thought made her feel happy, albeit tentatively so. The insights she had gained that day into Gladys's personality were beginning to sink into Aviva's mind, and she warmed to the thought of having Gladys as a friend. She would have to move carefully, though, allowing both herself and the older woman time to get used to what was becoming a new dimension to their relationship. She realized that this was probably the closest to an extended family she and Jenny would ever have, and she relished the idea, thankful that they had found such a wonderful friend in Tim and now in Gladys Barber, too. She couldn't help the little thought that a man to love would certainly make life a bit more perfect but quickly she tucked it away.

"Where's Jeremy? I want to have a business talk with him before dinner." Gladys's reed-thin voice broke through Aviva's reverie.

"Oh?" Aviva lifted her eyebrows curiously.

"I've got a little property in the valley. Thought he might be able to tell me what to do with it."

"Why should he tell you—" Aviva stopped short. It occurred to her that she had never really considered his business might extend to helping one person with her real estate. After all, he was involved in developing big, glamorous sites. Certainly, though, he had proved himself to be a friend to Gladys and he would help her if he could.

A telltale blush crept into her cheeks. Their intimacy had been complete; she knew the color of his eyes and the texture of the hair that ran across his broad chest, yet she had not really considered him in terms of his job. It seemed so useless, since that was a part of him she would never know. That was a part of the Los Angeles Jeremy.

His tender advances toward her, the talks, the jokes had all been designed to weave that web of intimacy, to keep her away from thoughts of the place she abhorred. She was sure that was why he never discussed his business in any great detail. She was almost sure the moment he returned to L.A. and people like Diane Chesterfield he would be singing a different tune. In Carmel people changed, became gentle. She didn't want to be around to see him become like the man Sam used to be. Aviva had come to cherish Jeremy too much to want to watch him revert to what she imagined he must be like down south.

"Don't tell me you don't even know what the man does for a living?" Mrs. Barber's demanding voice cut through the air like a knife. Before Aviva could answer, the old woman continued, "Why, the man builds buildings, hospitals and complexes, shopping centers, that kind of thing. Mighty bright, if you ask me," she finished as if she were a judge passing down sentence.

"Of course I knew, Gladys," Aviva answered, miffed at the older woman's lecture. Gladys, it seemed, would never get over her desire to point out the obvious and, to give her her due, Aviva was sure she had no idea why the topic seemed to be a sore one with Aviva. Now mad at herself for her reaction, Aviva hurried on, filling the conversation, "but I don't think you'll have much time to discuss anything in depth. He's going to be checking out in a few minutes."

"Well," Tim said casually, munching on the last of his carrot, "I guess things will get back to normal around here now."

"I guess they will," Aviva agreed almost to herself.

Gladys Barber shot a glance over her shoulder, her lips tightly clenched. Turning back to the caldron, she threw her two cents into the conversation. "Well, I know I'll miss him and so will Jenny. And I'll bet you a dime to a doughnut that there's someone else who'll be doing a little missing, too. It's a shame, if you ask me. People who are always trying to keep things the same. Looking at anything or anybody new as if there were some danger. People who are always protecting something when there really isn't anything to protect at all."

The two younger people stared at her. The impact of her words hung over the room like a cloud that has blocked the sun for a moment before moving on. They shrugged at each other behind her back, each denying the personal meaning of her words with their flippant attitude. Both Tim and Aviva wondered if the other knew what Gladys's comment had meant to the other, but neither let on.

For Aviva, the old woman had really hit the nail on the head, and she wondered if even Gladys was sure what her statement had meant. Whether or not she did, there was one thing that Aviva knew. She knew exactly what she was protecting: her sanity and safety, not to mention Jenny and the inn. The old woman had been standing over the hot stove too long. She really must learn to keep her opinions to herself at times.

"Well," Gladys said, putting the wooden spoon she had been using carefully on the porcelain caddy by the stove and wiping her hands on her apron, "I'm just going to go say good-bye to Jeremy. Somebody around here ought to be more than just civil."

Before Aviva could protest that Gladys's comment was unfair and unfounded, the older woman strode deliberately to the swinging door and disappeared through it, leaving Tim and Aviva to an uncomfortable silence.

A few moments later Aviva could hear hushed voices coming from near the dining room. Her curiosity was almost at the breaking point. Though she strained to make out what they were saying, she could only pick up a word here and there until she caught Mrs. Barber's parting call, "Don't give up, Jeremy."

In her heart Aviva knew they had been talking about her. Strangely, the idea did not seem to anger her as she knew it should. Was she looking for some way to make her relationship work with Jeremy even if it involved a feisty third party?

Aviva steeled herself, prepared to look into Jeremy's eyes once more, convinced that it would be for the last time. It was almost funny to think that at their last meeting she would be presenting him with a bill.

Her original determination to use him as word-of-mouth advertising so that she could pay her bills at the inn seemed so far away. The happiness he had brought her, the care he had shown her were worth far more than the price of a room. Loving him, looking at him, listening to him over the past week had brought him into the fold of her home. How could she charge him when he was so much a part of the house now? Smiling to herself, though, she realized that he would be far too disappointed in her if she didn't. Hadn't one of their first conversations been about the finer points of business?

Forcing herself to smile, denying the dull hurt that grew with each moment that brought his departure closer, Aviva pushed the kitchen door and walked into the dining room almost ready now to face him.

He must go soon, she thought as she moved forward, *or I know I will change my mind.*

But as her foot hit the carpeted floor when she entered the room she was surprised by his absence. Curious, she moved into the entryway. He was not to be found there, either. He couldn't have—wouldn't have—left without saying good-bye to her. Would he? No. His handsome, russet-colored leather bag had been placed neatly by the telephone alcove, the sheepskin coat thrown over it. Aviva's relief was instantaneous.

Like a child trying to steal a peek at the Christmas tree, Aviva stealthily crossed the Oriental rug and stopped in front of the living-room door. Feeling a bit ridiculous, she cautiously looked around the corner. He was there, on one knee in front of the settee where he had left Jenny.

As Aviva watched, the handsome man reached out his hand tentatively and stroked the little girl's long, unruly curls. Then, softly, he bent and kissed her forehead. Jenny did not move, did not wake. Only a faint smile played on her ruby cherub lips. Then, with the greatest care he rose and stood quietly beside the sleeping girl, careful not to make a sound, and looked down on the child with a tenderness that in some way did not really surprise Aviva.

Jeremy, Aviva thought sadly, aware that she was now almost beyond reason in love with him, yet knowing that reason was her only defense against him, *Jeremy, don't leave us, tell me that you love me enough to stay here with us. I'm not strong enough to try it your way yet.*

Her heart ached to have him come to her, engulf her in his arms, protect her and keep her safe. As if his heart heard hers calling out to him, he rose and turned to see her standing there. Aviva's lips parted in an effort to speak, but then, seeing the expression on his face, she stopped. Now he was not the handsome jester who had appeared at her door with a green plaid hat, nor was he the sensitive lover who had carefully brought her to his bed.

Jeremy was simply a man upon whose face a myriad of emotions played, leaping about, toying with his mind and heart. Aviva was shocked that mere flesh and blood could display such confusion, could be so easily read. How could she have any doubts about this man? Why didn't she simply speak now, tell him that she would go with him, follow him to the ends of the earth? Was it pride that made her stick to her resolve? Was it sheer stubbornness? Was she using Sam even now as an excuse for not giving Jeremy a chance, when it was her own fear of being hurt that kept her where she was?

Slowly Jeremy moved toward her. With each step Aviva felt her heart beat louder, keeping time with his movement until he stood before her and she knew that her heart must surely have stopped beating. Tentatively, his right hand moved as if to reach for her. Then, thinking more deeply, as if the mere touch of her skin would be too painful, it returned to his side, contact never made.

"Do you have my bill ready?" he whispered hoarsely, the words fairly pulling themselves out of his throat.

She nodded her assent, hesitated a moment, then turned away so that he could not see the mingling of disappointment and relief on her face. Disappointment because she yearned to touch him once more so that she could remember the warmth of his skin, the gentleness of his caress; relief because, had he dared to touch her, she could not have let him go. But what would she have done with him if he'd stayed? She could not keep him forever, hanging around like some pedigreed dog, ruining his spirit with her clinging if L.A. was where he wanted to be.

Making her way to the delicate desk that sat under the stairwell, Aviva rifled through the papers until she found the bill. Her hand wavered as she held it up to him. Though she did not look up, she could feel him coming toward her to stand so close that she could feel his body heat. Gently, he took the paper and her hand in his and drew both toward him until her arm was curled against his broad chest.

"I know, I know," he whispered his reassurance, "but I couldn't leave you without holding you one more time. I meant what I said, Aviva. This is not the end." Courageously, she looked into his eyes, feeling herself succumbing to the life in his body.

"A week is all I ask. Or a weekend, if that is all you'll let me have. Please don't judge me or my life-style without firsthand knowledge. Don't make decisions based on experiences that are long gone. Think of what we have had. Just think!" His voice was commanding and pleading all at the same time. Her mind and body were filled with the warmth of one who has been frozen and has been offered a welcoming fire but is afraid to go too close. His arms moved around her and she basked finally in the glow of their mutual love, pushing away her reservations for just one last brief moment.

"Cherry, wait a minute." Suddenly their moment was broken as the dog burst into the hall and sandwiched itself between their legs. Jumping back from each other when they heard Tim's call, they looked down at the red, wiggling creature between them.

An instant later Tim was rushing into the room after the dog. Seeing Aviva and Jeremy, reading their faces, Tim was suddenly silent and at a loss for words.

"Hey, Aviva—I'm—" he stuttered, his own cheeks burning with an unaccustomed blush. "I, well, I know you don't want the dog in here...." Feeling odd man out to the greatest degree, Tim simply caught the dog by the collar and dragged it out behind him, making no further attempt at apology.

Aviva and Jeremy watched him go, then turning

back to each other, stared for a moment before Aviva started to giggle. Jeremy followed suit, his deep laughter a perfect foil for hers.

"The bill comes to $416 for the four nights you were with us, Mr. Crowley," Aviva said through her chuckles. "And that includes the phone calls," she finished, now almost fully in control of her mirth.

"Well worth it, Mrs. Thompson," Jeremy countered, adding a mock bow. Straightening, he faced her once more and reiterated with great feeling, "well worth it, Aviva."

He gathered her once more in his arms, and they stood there, each lost in their own thoughts in the comfort and satisfaction of each other's body. Gently he kissed the top of her head, which rested on his shoulder. Then, holding her at arm's length, he looked deep into her eyes. A soft, slow smile spread across his face as if he had found the answer to some question of great import. Retrieving his bag and coat he headed toward the heavy oak door. As he turned, his eyes bore into hers, swept over her one last time.

"See you soon, Aviva. Tell Jenny the same." With that confident statement he was gone and Aviva thought her heart would break, falling into a thousand pieces for all to see. But nothing had changed. The inn was still there, in the gathering dusk and fog, among the cypress trees. No, nothing really important had changed. The fire just wouldn't be as warm, the books on the table a little less interesting and the nights just a tad bit longer. But it was a small price to pay for her safety, for Jenny's safety.

The sound of Jeremy's engine was almost beyond

hearing when Tim's timid voice came from behind her.

"Aviva? Is he gone?" Without turning she nodded.

"Look," he went on when she didn't answer, "I'm really sorry about the interruption. Cherry and I just got to playing and he got so excited he tore off before I had a chance to catch him."

"It's okay, Tim, no harm done." Aviva straightened her shoulders and turned to face her companion. A brave smile adorned her face, and Tim felt ill at ease in front of her.

"Aviva," Tim said, fidgeting with his fingers, "was it really that hard?"

"No, Tim," she lied, "but thanks for asking."

"Well, then," Tim said, "why don't you go clean up, take a long hot bath, and I'll set the table for dinner. By the time you come down everything will be taken care of."

Aviva nodded her assent. As she checked Jenny and headed up the stairs she could hear Tim whistling softly in the dining room. Her tears fell freely as she lounged in the warm bathwater. She felt no shame for her quiet mourning but she did feel unsettled by the impact Jeremy had had on her. If she felt strongly enough to cry over him, then should she have gone with him? But one major disappointment, one giant hurt in life was enough. Better to enjoy the happiness at hand than to take a chance on ruining it by taking risks.

Her tears finally spent, she lay for a while in the soothing, scented warmth of the tub. Then, rising, she dressed for dinner feeling somewhat relieved after the release of her sorrow and confusion. She was so mixed up. Loving yet not wanting to feel. Yet it didn't matter anymore. Jeremy was gone.

Dinner was a quiet affair. All of the guests were out except for Mr. Fortman, and he had requested dinner in his room. Jenny had awakened from her long nap grumpy, demanding to know where Jeremy had gone and why he hadn't said good-bye to her. Aviva had explained that Jeremy had said good-bye, but she didn't want to tell Jenny about the kiss and his gentle farewell to her, fearing it would raise her hopes for his return.

Tim had been more animated than Aviva had ever seen him. Just that day he had received another commission for an extremely intricate window, the project completely banishing his earlier disappointment. Unfortunately, as he attempted to describe the convoluted waves and curls that he would incorporate into the piece, he knocked over one of the Waterford goblets, sending it crashing into the oak hutch.

Pushing back her chair roughly, Aviva retrieved the broken crystal. It was beyond repair, and she could not hide her immediate and icy anger from the others at the table.

Everyone was shocked by Aviva's sudden change of mood, including Aviva herself. She knew she shouldn't let her sadness at Jeremy's leaving and her anger that he didn't think of staying with her interfere with the normal comings and goings at the inn. But she couldn't preside at the dinner table as she usually did, for she felt his absence too keenly.

"You know," Gladys Barber began when the silence had grown too long and too heavy, "the doors are still sticking. I think you're going to have to have them cut down again. Just a little. Shouldn't take your man long."

"I'd noticed," Aviva answered, with a lilt in her voice.

"Well?" Gladys pressed for more specifics.

Aviva raised her eyes to meet the old woman's and attempted a smile. "Well, I'll talk to the contractor when I go into town tomorrow," Aviva offered, lowering her eyes to her plate once more as the silence fell again.

The dinner progressed with stilted talk, and finally the gloomy meal came to an end. Gladys, in a display of generosity and understanding that seemed to be the order of the day, offered to take care of the dishes and put Jenny to bed. Tim disappeared almost immediately, much to Aviva's relief, explaining he had a lot of work to do on the new job.

Left alone, Aviva wandered into the living room and poured herself a glass of wine, enjoying the crystal clarity of the liquid as she turned her glass in front of the dim light. Shivering, she realized there was no fire burning and moved to put a few logs on the grate. Then, stopping, she raised herself to her full height, dusting her hand on the side of her trousers as she did so. For a moment she stared into the dark cavern of the old stone fireplace.

Jeremy wouldn't be with her that night. She didn't want to be alone in the room that had so recently been the stage for such pleasant evenings. She didn't want a fire to blaze more brightly than her memories of those

YOURS FREE

4 Harlequin American Romances™ and a fashion tote

It's our way of introducing you to our Harlequin Reader Service that's so much easier and less expensive than buying your novels retail.

As a subscriber, you'll receive 4 new books to preview every month. Always before they're available in stores. Always for the same low price. Always with the right to return the shipment and owe nothing.

AR2TMU

►►► FREE BOOKS & TOTE BAG ◄◄◄

nights. Turning away, Aviva crossed to the window and gently pulled back the long lace drape thinking that perhaps she should do some bookkeeping. But knowing that her mind could not concentrate on the cold figures, she discarded the idea. Outside, everything was quiet. The March winds had decided to rest, and the fog, though evident, was lighter than Aviva had ever seen it. Aviva moved toward the French doors that led to the veranda and stepped out.

The cool night air grabbed her, held her close and then, when she had become used to the dampness around her, released her in comfort. She went down the cornflower-blue steps she had painted only two weeks earlier and walked toward the beach.

Though familiar to her, the surroundings seemed different: comforting, but lacking the intensity she had once found on her land. Slowly she walked, sometimes losing her balance slightly as she encountered a sudden, slight rift or mound in the ground beneath her. Her free hand caressed the tall grass, which parted easily to let her pass, while with the other she cradled her wineglass, careful not to spill any of the warming liquid.

Above her the stars glimmered like so many sugar crystals sprinkled over a chocolate Christmas cookie by a loving hand. She had reached the end of the wild grass; it stopped suddenly, as if in respect for the beauty that lay before it, unwilling to trespass onto the smooth white sand that stretched toward the ocean like the porcelain face of a sleeping woman.

Here and there on the slope of a dune, a small shrub would valiantly attempt to grow, peeking its withered form out from under layers of white grains for one last look at the ever-changing sea before the evening wind would reshape the lay of the dunes and cover the little plant.

Aviva stopped, removed her kilties and stepped onto the velvet sand. Sinking into its depths she waited, acquainting herself with the new territory before she proceeded.

Then the sea was before her. Tonight, the ocean, like her emotions, was calm on the outside but the raging, pounding surf of the past weeks still lingered underneath the quiet surface. Though abated, the power had only retreated into the great depths to regather its strength before rearing its majestic force once again to assault the wild coastline of Northern California.

Over and over again she questioned the wisdom of her decision regarding Jeremy. She felt so much like the sea: dark, glassy smooth, ready to be broken apart by outside forces.

Aviva watched carefully, counting the seconds between the wave's movements. Only when the great mass reached the shore did the water swell gently and reach out to caress the sands, pulling its white, foamy fingers across the face of the land like a lover touching his sleeping partner. The sound, a whisper cajoling a lover to even deeper dreams or loving wakefulness, whichever was meant to be, for the lover was generous in his desire.

Aviva settled herself back to watch the black night, careless of her gabardine slacks and freshly washed hair. Closing her eyes, she let the night play about her like some precocious elf. The water lapped at her toes, the breeze caressed her face, and the sand shifted to mold to her body.

The intermittent movement of her hand to raise her wineglass was the only activity of her entire being. Her mind had stopped thinking its torturous thoughts. Yet as the images persisted and passed through her, she did not tarry long enough to grasp any one of them.

Thoughts of Jenny and Jeremy, Tim and Gladys, all whirled about her head. She was tired of caring so deeply, of fighting a battle she could not remember starting. For tonight she would simply let them all be there—with her but not a part of her.

Finally she rose to return to the darkened house. Blissfully, the sounds of the night had finally, completely swept the images from her head. When, she did not remember; she only knew that for a time she had been released from thoughts of love and caring and responsibility. Aviva felt strangely content and refreshed. The crystal glass lay at her side, and she reached down to retrieve it. A last drop of wine remained and she considered it for an instant.

"Is it better to finish it?" she mused, "drink deep and have done with it? Or should one simply be grateful for what one has already tasted and not search for the last satisfying drop?"

Philosophy! She had never been very good at it. Tonight, she would leave it. Tipping the glass, she let the last bit of wine fall to the sands, where it was accepted, disappearing and leaving only a darkened spot as remembrance.

Aviva had not put her shoes back on and entered the house silently by the back door. Locking it, she made her way through the quiet house, noting as she passed that Gladys was still up. She climbed the stairs to check on her daughter. Jenny slept, snugly covered by the quilt, but stirred as Aviva reached down to kiss her warm cheek.

"Mommy?" The sleepy voice reached out to her. "Can I write a letter to Jeremy?"

Aviva smiled gently, sweetly, at her daughter. Reaching down, she stroked the little girl's hair. "Sleep now, my darling," she whispered. "We'll talk about it in the morning."

Before she had even finished the sentence Jenny was once again deep in sleep's spell. With one last look of love Aviva left her daughter to her dreams, knowing that Jeremy would be included not only in Jenny's but in hers, also.

In her own room Aviva was restless. She paced back and forth, stopping now and then to retrieve a gown from the armoire or loosen her hair from the confining barettes. Settling herself at the dressing table she brushed through the heavy tresses that ran down her back. Midstroke she stopped and gently put the brush on the mirrored tray. Hesitantly, she reached for the right-hand drawer and opened it slowly.

Riffling through the silk slips that were neatly folded, she found what she was looking for. The pictures. Carefully she pulled them from their hiding place and cocked their stands, setting them upright before her.

From one surrounded by burgundy leather Sam

looked out at her, smiling as if in greeting. His eyes danced, asking why she had kept him hidden so long. He was happy to see the world again, if only the confines of her bedroom.

The other photo was encased in a simple brass-plated frame, long since tarnished and worn. The medium-height man with the dark wavy hair stood by an old-fashioned motorcycle. The picture was the only way she had ever known her father. He had disappeared when she was only four. He was anxious to keep living, and living didn't include a wife and child. At least Sam had stayed physically close. Yet she couldn't find it in her heart to hate either one of them. Nor could she understand their behavior. It was simply the way they were.

Now, as the pictures stood side by side, Aviva looked from one to the other comparing, searching the faces for similarities. Both men were extraordinarily handsome. The camera had captured the intense sparkle in each of them, the sparkle that comes from constant movement, impatience, charm.

Aviva's head rose slightly. There had been a noise. It sounded again: a soft knock at her door. It couldn't be Jenny; she would simply have come through the connecting door. Maybe one of her guests needed something. Crossing the room silently, Aviva opened the whitewashed door. Mrs. Barber stood before her, a quilted pink dressing gown buttoned tightly to her throat, a thin hair net gathered over her bun and caught with a small metal clip on her forehead. She looked so vulnerable.

"Gladys, is everything all right? Are you ill?"

Aviva asked, suddenly alert, all other worries shoved from her mind.

"Hardly." The old woman entered the room without an invitation. "Nice room. Maybe I should have taken this one." Aviva closed the door, confused and unnerved as always by Gladys's forthright manner.

"Thought you'd like to talk... woman to woman if you know what I mean." It was a statement, almost an order to Aviva to pour her heart out, but she was not going to be taken in. Despite Gladys's help that day, Aviva was still wary of the woman.

"There's really not much to talk about," she lied, half wanting to ask the old woman what she should do. But how would she know the answers that Aviva sought so desperately? Surely she had been removed from affairs of the heart long ago, and her manner did not exactly invite personal conversation.

"I don't believe that for a second, young woman. The way you behaved at dinner tonight, even a blind man would know you've got a lot on your mind. Happy as a clam one minute, then bitin' our heads off and mopin' around like a spoiled child the next." She had settled herself on the princess chair next to the dressing table and was arranging her robe to cover her knit slippers.

"Now—" her voice softened, sounding unusual coming from the withered lips "—why don't we talk about Jeremy?"

For a long while Aviva simply watched Gladys Barber. Like a Mexican standoff the two women stared into each other's eyes. Then something in Aviva told her to take a chance. Perhaps Gladys was worth taking a chance on. Amazed at her own sudden acquiescence, Aviva returned to the stool by her dressing table and began to talk.

The words poured out, and it was a relief to her even knowing that Mrs. Barber could never understand how deeply she had been hurt and how hard it was for her to trust any man—including Jeremy—or cast her fortune with someone else again. She even went so far as to tell the woman that she had fallen in love with him. Aviva tried to explain why she couldn't allow herself to get involved, but the words just wouldn't express what she was feeling.

"Isn't it really because of those two?" Gladys indicated the pictures still standing on the dressing table after Aviva had finished. "Is that why you think you've got to cut yourself off in the prime of your life? Just because you got hurt once or twice getting to where you are now?"

She hadn't expected the woman to understand. "Yes," she answered patiently. "I loved my husband and I probably adored my father when he was around, but they were both the same—impossibly attentive only when it suited them. I haven't seen much to make me think differently about any other man, even Jeremy." Even to Aviva the words sounded hollow, defensive and self-serving. But she knew what was best for her and she wasn't going to let anyone tell her differently.

Gladys motioned for Aviva to hand her the pictures, which she did reluctantly. The woman drew on a pair of glasses and looked down her nose at the images.

"You are a coward, Missy. That's what you are." The words were like a slap to Aviva. How dare Gladys speak to her like that? She opened her mouth to answer, but Gladys continued on. "Now, I'm going to tell you a couple of things. First, those were two good men. A little different from the normal man, but then the normal man is kind of boring. You were lucky to have known them." She removed her glasses and folded her hands on her lap. "Next, I wouldn't bet that Jeremy Crowley is exactly like them. Sure, he has a little of the devil in him but he's got a lot of caring in him, too. Would you want him if all he did was moon around you all day?" Aviva lowered her eyes, knowing full well she wouldn't but not wanting to admit it.

"Now, the most important thing I have to tell you is that my name isn't Mrs. Barber. I know young people don't think old people have any real experiences worth hearing about but I think you'll understand this one.

"I'm just plain old *Miss* Barber. But when I came here I thought if I called myself Mrs. it would lend an air of respectability that I had always wanted.

"When I was younger than you, my lady, I loved a man like the ones in your pictures there. I loved him so much I would have died for him. In fact, I guess I did just a little." She sighed and then continued, her eyes meeting Aviva's defiantly. "Well, to make a long story short, he stood me up on our wedding day. Just plain scared, I guess. After that I wouldn't have anything to do with men.

"Oh, I was a hard one, but there were still plenty who wanted me, believe it or not." She paused for a moment and fished her lace handkerchief out of her deep pocket. She held it to her nose, blew, then returned it to her pocket. It was such an uncharacteristic gesture that Aviva smiled to herself.

"Well, anyway, one day I woke up old, realizing that I had missed out on something special. I might have been hurt again but it would have been worth it just to feel a little life in me. I wasn't always this nice, you know." Aviva smiled at the crusty lady, feeling tears welling up in her own eyes, experiencing a new respect for Gladys Barber.

"When I moved here it was too late. You know, packaging is pretty important and by that time you could say the bloom was definitely off the rose. Anyway, I came to Carmel and wove a story that I was a married lady. But I don't think respectability was the real reason I did it. I think I just wanted to remind myself of my stupidity. I had let the best part of my life escape me because I had been so bullheaded.

She was fighting her emotions now, showing herself to be more sensitive than she would have liked Aviva to believe as she finished. "Now, you just think about that story. You don't have to call me a silly old woman because I know that already."

Yes, Aviva thought to herself, *I had thought you a silly old miserable woman whom no one could please.* How wrong she had been! Gladys was simply an older version of herself: confused and disappointed by what life had given her.

Aviva rose with Gladys Barber and put her hand out, stopping the woman before she could reach the door. She wanted to apologize for all the terrible

thoughts she had had about Gladys. Aviva wanted her
to know how much she appreciated her sharing such a
secret. But no words would come, so Aviva simply
bent down and gave her a gentle hug before she disappeared into the darkened hall.

Closing the door, she leaned against it for an instant, contemplating the story of Gladys's life. Aviva
knew that the woman had only told her the story
thinking it would help her. Gladys had known all
along about her growing feelings for Jeremy and probably felt a responsibility to help the romance along
the road. After all, she was a permanent part of the
house and, it seemed, a family member as she saw her
role; like any concerned family member, she wanted
to help any way she could. How ashamed Aviva felt of
her earlier dislike for Gladys!

But Gladys had failed to consider that times were
different. The world in which a man and woman existed today was so much more complicated than it had
been in her time. And Aviva's situation was entirely
different. She had married. She had borne Jenny, who
now filled her life with such happiness it was beyond
description. What would Gladys have said if her
gentleman friend had married and then deserted her?
Would her words of wisdom be the same?

Slowly Aviva moved over to the window and
looked out into the night. She was unable to deny,
however, the one very strong lesson that Gladys had
taught her: One did grow old and lonely. If Aviva were
to continue as she was, commiting herself to Whaler's
Inn, what would happen? Jenny would grow up, go to
school, work, then probably marry. Of course, she

would still have a daughter but it would not be the same.

Aviva might not be as lucky as Gladys to find a family who would not only take her into their home in her later years but also into their hearts. Was Jeremy her only chance? If he was, then perhaps she should take it without regard to the dangers he posed to the happiness she had made for herself.

Suddenly tired from all the contemplation, Aviva turned toward the bed. It would feel good to sleep. The sheets rustled comfortingly as she turned them back, got into the high bed and covered herself.

Closing her eyes, she attempted to sleep. But, as is often the case, the harder she concentrated on sleep the faster thoughts of Jeremy and the wakefulness that accompanied them came. Even now, alone in her bed, her pulse quickened as she remembered the caresses of their night of love, the warmth of his kisses, the touch of his hand on her waist, her neck, her hips.

But then as her unbidden reactions peaked, the memories became hazy dreams. Aviva found herself drifting off into blessed sleep, a contented smile playing about her lips. Then, just as she was about to cross the threshold into the regions of darkness that would hold her fast until morning light, she was startled by the muted ringing of the phone beside her bed.

Her arm snaked out from under the quilt and she had only a moment to bless her foresight, thanking herself for at least putting an extension in her room so she didn't have to run down the long flight of stairs to the phone in the alcove. Attempting to sound alert in case it was a potential client, Aviva spoke into the receiver.

"Hello, Whaler's Inn." Unfortunately, sleep had taken too deep a hold and her voice was fuzzy, low and sensual as she spoke. There was a moment of silence from the other end and finally her caller answered.

"I couldn't sleep without saying good night." Jeremy's voice wafted through the phone lines over the hundreds of miles that separated them, and Aviva snuggled deeper into the pillows, waiting for him to speak once more. His voice was like a lullaby, and she thought no more of the concerns of the day.

"I love you, Aviva. Sleep well, my love." With that the phone went dead. Aviva fell asleep cradling the receiver.

Chapter Six

Sue was already busy with breakfast when Aviva entered the kitchen. Her manner was brisk and efficient as she checked on the preparations, her smile quick and genuine each time she addressed the young girl.

The weeks that had passed since Jeremy's departure had brought about an unexpected attitude in Aviva, and everyone from the mailman to Mrs. Barber was pleased with the outcome. Jeremy's first call that late night so long ago had seemed but a pleasant dream when Aviva had awakened the next morning. As if making a New Year's resolution, she had decided then and there that surely she had dreamed the lovely words and she would not think of him again. Her decision had been made and even Gladys's well-intentioned words would not sway her. Aviva would continue with life as it was before Jeremy Crowley's arrival.

But later that day, as Aviva moved about the house completing her chores, greeting guests and making out bills for those who were leaving, a delivery boy had brought her an armful of yellow roses. The note

read simply, "Our nights should be shared. Jeremy."
So, she realized, she had not dreamed the call.

Touched as she was by his thoughtfulness, Aviva
knew that it was simply a romantic gesture on his part.
Jeremy was still mentally living in Carmel, tired from
the long drive back to Los Angeles. He was a dear,
and Aviva felt a pang of longing as she buried her
nose in the beautiful bouquet, wondering how much
it would hurt when he no longer called her in the wee
hours of the morning, when she finally realized that
her assessment of the situation had been correct all
along. When Jeremy Crowley proved to be exactly
what she had expected.

Even as she pondered the question she knew what
the answer would be. Of course it would hurt terribly.
No amount of logical thinking could prevent that. She
loved him, the man he had been when he was with
her, and nothing would change that. What she must
do, though, was to put him in the proper perspective
when the pain came.

Naturally, the enormous bouquet of roses brought
comment from Tim and Jenny and Gladys, but Aviva
gracefully put an end to all conversation regarding Jeremy as soon as it arose.

Aviva had been the only one surprised when the
phone calls did not desist and the flowers kept coming
until the inn looked like a florist's shop. After a week
and a half of deliveries Aviva finally had to ask Jeremy to stop his improbable courting.

"Jeremy," she had said, exasperated but nonetheless pleased by the attention, "you've got to stop
this."

"What?" Jeremy played the injured party to the hilt, and it had made Aviva giggle.

"You know what. All these flowers. I could be wrong, but maybe I died and this is my funeral."

"Aviva, the flowers are only a token of my undying affection," he had protested, still teasing her, but she could hear the sincerity in his words.

"Jeremy, I'm serious. It must be costing you a fortune." Desperately she tried to be firm but she knew the argument would hold no water so she forged ahead. "Besides, all this attention is giving Jenny the wrong idea. She keeps thinking that you're going to pop up any minute and things will be as they were."

"Well, you just tell Jenny that since I enjoyed your hospitality it's time you enjoyed mine," Jeremy said tentatively, the invitation hanging in the air once again. When Aviva was silent he had forced his voice to brighten again as he changed the subject. "By the way, did I tell you that I clinched the deal for the first shopping center on Rodeo?"

"No," Aviva said, grateful for the change in tack but irked by the mention of the Hills. How easily she could imagine Jeremy flitting about, lunching and playing with the beautiful people. That was the Jeremy she imagined to be real, not the one who spoke to her so sweetly over the phone. Still, he must be very proud of such an accomplishment and she couldn't dispel his happiness because of her own prejudice. "That's great, Jeremy. I'm sure you'll make it beautiful."

"I hope so. There's a lot riding on this one. Everyone who is anyone will be watching me. It could lead to a lot more contracts. And the best part is that I've managed to make a wholesale deal with one of the most important stores in the entire complex."

"That's nice," Aviva responded.

"Don't you want to know which one?" Jeremy pressed, obviously excited by his deal.

"Yes. I'm sorry. Of course I do."

"Fred's. You know, the jeweler. I could lay my hands on the most fabulous diamond for a pittance. Would that sway you at all?" Jeremy asked, laughingly. "I mean, it shows how practical I can be, and I know how much that quality means to you."

"Jeremy, you're crazy." Aviva verbally reprimanded him, all the while blushing at the idea of an engagement ring.

"Crazy in love. I miss you so much." His tone was serious and Aviva was at a loss for words. She was crazy in love, too, but his idea of practicality and hers were different. He would simply have to realize that.

"We miss you, too, Jeremy," she answered noncommittally. At the other end of the phone Aviva heard a deep sigh and she knew she had hurt him.

"Well, I'm glad you include yourself in that statement. But I'm not going to give up. Believe that. I've never lost before. I won't lose now." She knew he meant what he said. If nothing else, he was persistent. Yet one of these days he would realize that she was right in her decision. One of these days he would wonder why he had even bothered with the lady in Carmel.

The conversation had been mundane after that. Aviva tried to keep it light, filling him in on the everyday goings on at the inn and Jeremy, too, responded in kind. Finally, reluctantly, he had promised to heed her wishes about the flowers, told her he would call again soon and rung off, leaving Aviva to begin missing him all over again.

So the flowers had stopped coming once a day and for the next three weeks they arrived only every Friday. But the phone calls had persisted. Aviva had tried to remain bright, friendly but removed during the calls. But with each successive one her heart grew softer, her longing more evident. Jeremy did not push the idea of a visit to L.A. Instead, it seemed that their chats were simply extensions of the ones they had enjoyed in front of the fireplace at Whaler's Inn. Even though he did not press her, the conversation always concluded with a hint of what they would do if she ever came to see him.

Even his letters caused her heart to pound, her pulse to race as she read them over and over again in the privacy of her own room. Her mind could hear the soft sweetness of his voice, the quick laughter that she knew would have accompanied a sentence had he been there to speak it.

Her love grew, her longing expanded with each passing day as he continued his gentle long-distance courtship. The one night they had spent together, the last lingering embrace before he left had not faded into memory but seemed to grow more glorious each time she reflected upon them.

The household was happy as Jeremy's specter continued to watch over them, and everyone wondered when the man would again appear at their door, when the long-distance relationship between them would settle itself once and for all. Even Aviva knew that they could not go on like this indefinitely, and more than once she berated herself for encouraging his advances, although she tried to convince herself that she was simply retaining a beautiful friendship and no more.

Now as she moved about the kitchen, Aviva knew that she would have to make a decision one way or the other: completely release Jeremy from her life or take a chance that what they had could transcend her fears. Go to visit him as he asked.

There were two more days until the end of the week. That was the deadline she had given herself. If nothing had changed by then, if Jeremy continued to call, then she would make up her mind and tell him her decision, her final decision.

Even now, though, Aviva knew that the deadline was artificial. There was more than an intellectual decision to be made. There was the insistence of both her body and soul that she see Jeremy again, be held once more against his broad chest, feel his gentle breathing, his lips upon hers. As much as she wanted to deny it Aviva could not ignore the call of physical love any more than she could disavow her mental longing.

But having given herself until the end of the week to make that final decision, Aviva somehow felt safe. The extra days were like a buffer between what she knew she would do and what she knew she should do.

Putting thoughts of Jeremy and her impending decision out of her mind, she turned toward Sue, who had addressed her.

"I'm sorry, Sue, what did you say?" Aviva inquired, flustered that she had been so lost in thought.

"Room six was taken this morning as soon as I got here, Mrs. Thompson," the girl said shyly, a note of pride in her voice. Aviva was not unaware that Sue was happy working for her, and she intended to offer her permanent employment very soon.

"That's great. Who is it?" Aviva responded, genuinely pleased.

"An older couple, Mr. and Mrs. Jenkins. It's their fiftieth wedding anniversary. They'll be here a week. Maybe…" The sturdy girl looked up. Aviva knew that she stood ten feet tall in Sue's eyes and smiled brightly at her. "Maybe we could fix a special dinner tonight or something for them?" she suggested, biting her upper lip in anticipation of the answer.

"I think that would be a great idea. Would you like to do it on your own or do you want some help?"

"Oh, on my own, Mrs. Thompson." Sue nodded enthusiastically. Her eyes shone as if she had just been given the biggest responsibility in the whole world. "I won't let you down."

"I know you won't. You never do. In the meantime make sure that there are fresh flowers in their room every day and see if they'll need anything special." As an afterthought she added, "Oh, and why don't you put them in room seven if they want to move. There's a fireplace in there and you could bring some wood up for them. They might like a fire, considering this is a very special time for them."

Aviva smiled to herself as Sue rushed out of the room to see to the change. Fiftieth wedding anniversary, she mused. It seemed everywhere she looked these days there was something to remind her that there were people who enjoyed each other for years: happily married couples, people holding hands on the street or whispering over a cup of coffee in the cafés. Why, even her own inn had entertained what seemed to be happily married couples. Then, with a sigh, Aviva reminded herself that things were not always as they seemed.

But as she pushed herself away from the counter she had been leaning on, a little voice reminded her that there was always reason to hope that happiness could be hers, too. The emptiness she had denied before she met Jeremy Crowley had simply become more pronounced since his departure. Aviva was more aware of herself as a healthy, attractive woman with desires she should not be ashamed of. She was even more aware of the fact that Jeremy seemed to be the one who could fill the void.

Tousling her hair in order to clear her thoughts, she made her way to the foyer, picking up the mail as she went. Glancing through it she settled herself at the little desk. Bills, bills and more bills. Thankfully, there was no reason to put any of them off, though it meant she would not be doing any extravagant spending.

A surge of pride gripped her and she let her eyes roam over the room in which she sat. She had done it! The inn was running in the black and she was the one responsible. Her friends were true blue and stalwart, and even Jenny was happier than she had ever been before.

Life had been so good to her, Lady Luck had never left her perch on Aviva's shoulder, so why did the desire to go to Jeremy grow with each passing day, each phone call and every new batch of flowers from him?

Quickly, she opened the desk drawer and withdrew the checkbook and the pearl-gray stationery. In a few moments she had dutifully written and recorded the checks, put them in their respective envelopes, sealed and stamped them and set them in neat little piles.

Moving the stationery toward her, she settled down to her favorite task of the day—writing thank-you notes to those who had recently vacated their rooms. Part of her success, she knew, was derived from her extremely personal service. From the cordials before dinner to the Whaler's Inn thank-you notes, Aviva planned and executed her business dealings with a touch of the romantic, and people reciprocated by passing along the name of her establishment and promising to come back.

Before she could put pen to paper, though, Jenny burst into the room disturbing the wonderful peace Aviva needed to compose her notes so that no two were the same.

"Hi, Mommy." The little girl stood on tiptoe to greet her mother with a kiss. Behind her Cherry bounded about the room only to end up nuzzling Aviva, jealous of the attention Jenny was getting. The dog was getting so big he would soon be larger than Jenny. Then, reaching down to pet the glossy red fur,

Aviva remembered the day Jeremy had brought him home. The man really was a kid at heart, she thought, his smiling face as he presented the dog coming to mind again.

"Want to see what Gladys and I taught Cherry?" Jenny queried, her little voice excited.

"Of course I do," Aviva responded, her heart suddenly filled with love for the little girl who stood before her so self-sufficiently.

As Jenny and Cherry moved back a few paces Aviva thanked God that Gladys was so fond of dogs and knew how to handle them. Cherry was becoming quite the perfect pet. He had been housebroken in a matter of days, and the only thing he had ever destroyed had been six pork chops Aviva had carelessly left out on the counter to defrost. Though she had been mad at the dog, she really couldn't blame him. The temptation had just been too great.

"Okay, Mommy. Now watch." Jenny raised her hand, palm down and Cherry watched it intently. Quickly, Jenny's hand cut down to rest at her side, and immediately Cherry dropped to the floor, his muzzle wedged between his long legs. Jenny then put her hand out as if she were a crossing guard, looked at her mother, then turned and ran out of the room.

For a few minutes Cherry remained where he was, watching the door through which Jenny had disappeared. Finally, the pup could resist it no longer and went in search of his little mistress. A squeal erupted from the other room as the dog found his happy prey, and Aviva could hear Jenny berating him for not staying. Poor Cherry, he wouldn't know what to do with himself when Jenny went to school the following year.

Soon the two reappeared in front of Aviva. "Well, he *almost* knows how to do it," Jenny said, exasperated.

"I think he did just fine," Aviva said, giving his head a pat. "Why don't you take him outside. There's no fog and it's almost warm today. You can practice some more with him. Just don't go too far." In an instant they were gone.

Thinking about the day ahead Aviva wondered if she would have time for their play hour. The day was going to be packed, what with the shopping trip, which had become a weekly event for Gladys and Aviva since the two women had become friends. Well, she would just have to get those notes out fast and make the time. Turning back to the desk she applied herself to her task until two hours later when Gladys appeared, purse in hand, ready for their trek into town.

"Ready to go?" she inquired curtly, her dry smile belying the harshness of her inquiry.

"Just about," Aviva answered. "Would you mind putting the stamps on these while I get my coat and purse? Then we can drop them off at the post office while we're in town."

"Be happy to," Gladys said, settling herself in the chair Aviva had just vacated. Funny how their late-night talk had sealed a bargain between the two women. Aviva no longer felt as if Gladys were trying to take over the running of the house. Now she welcomed the help as much as Gladys enjoyed giving it.

Quickly Aviva made her way upstairs. Glancing at herself in the mirror before she reached for her coat, she noted her appearance with approval. She fairly sparkled and wondered if Jeremy's constant long-distance attention had anything to do with it. She had dressed casually for the day, preferring to be comfortable as they hiked up and down the main street, knowing they would stop at every store.

Her long legs were encased in velvety corduroy jeans of cornflower blue. Over them she had pulled a bulky sweater, subtle in stripes of beige, blue and rose. Its giant turtleneck collar was big enough for her to bury her chin in should the wind act up on the bright day.

Finally she had pulled on a pair of low-heeled English riding boots, the small gold insignia of Bally their only adornment. Her hair fell loose and clean, parted down the middle of her head. She felt exceedingly lighthearted and almost decided not to bring a jacket. Then knowing it would be better to be safe than sorry, she grabbed a light one.

The outings with Gladys had really added a new dimension to her life. What with Sue helping her, Gladys's growing friendship and Jenny's happiness with Cherry as her companion, Aviva felt that her life in Carmel had settled into a delightful routine. If only Jeremy would come, let them progress in that atmosphere, she knew how much easier it would be for her.

Grabbing her purse, Aviva headed down the stairs, past Gladys, who was putting the last of the stamps on the notes, and made her way through the kitchen.

Opening the door an inch, she saw Cherry and Jenny practicing their new trick in the field.

"Jenny, Mrs. Barber and I are going now," she yelled, her voice carrying easily in the crystal-clear air.

"Okay, Mommy," the child yelled back, accompanied by a woof from Cherry.

"Be good for Sue" was Aviva's parting warning before she closed the door and turned to Sue, who was now cleaning the kitchen to its normal spotless beauty.

"Anything you need from town?" Aviva asked. .

"No, but you may want to restock the candles. We've been going through them awfully fast. Maybe we shouldn't burn so many."

"Oh, but I just love candlelight, don't you?" Aviva said, grateful for Sue's concern but knowing she would never give up the romance of candlelight in the public rooms.

"Oh, yes. I just thought if you were looking for ways to cut down on costs..." Her words trailed off.

"Don't worry, Sue. We're doing just fine, but I appreciate your concern. In fact, I'd like to talk to you about your position here real soon." Sue's suddenly frantic look made Aviva feel guilty the moment she saw it and she spoke quickly to allay any fears the girl might have. "Oh, Sue, I just meant you are doing such a good job I thought we might expand your responsibilities."

Instantly, Sue's face dropped back into its normally happy expression. "I'd like that. Thank you, Mrs. Thompson."

"Do you think you could try calling me Aviva?"

"Oh, yes. Thank you," Sue responded, blushing with delight.

"Good. Now, we'll be gone until about two, so just watch out for Jenny, if you don't mind." With that she was gone.

"Well," Gladys said as Aviva reappeared, "are we going to get this show on the road or would you rather stay here all day?"

"I'm ready when you are," she answered, walking to the door and holding it open as Gladys breezed through. Aviva smiled. Every week it was the same. Gladys dressed in her Sunday best for their shopping adventure. The costume never changed: soft beige coat, of good quality but many years, buttoned up to her chin, the little mink collar framing her face; a matching fur hat perched on her bun; a pair of white cloth gloves buttoned at the wrist; and low-heeled black shoes that laced up the front. Nun shoes Aviva used to call them when she was a kid.

The two women headed out the door, and Aviva chuckled as Gladys fought to settle herself in the bucket seat of the VW.

"Isn't like the old days, when cars were made for people to stretch out in," she muttered. But now Aviva took only amused notice of her complaints, knowing that Gladys was pleased at having something to grouse about. Thank goodness Aviva had learned that Gladys was human, too. She had needed a friend and the old woman filled the bill perfectly, if you could get around her caustic nature and see the real, delightful Gladys underneath.

The drive was lovely. Carmel appeared gradually as

one approached it from the scenic drive. Slowly the wild grass and cypress trees gave away to low Spanish-style stucco bungalows nestled in the overgrowth. Then before one was really aware they were there, the road became a wide avenue and the cottages were closer together, still buffered by the trees; but the scent that filled the air was eucalyptus. They stood tall and straight, unlike the low, molded shapes of cypress.

Hardly a car was to be seen, and Aviva imagined the men and women who lived in Carmel tucked safely behind the front doors of the houses, enjoying the fireplace, maybe painting or sewing or simply reading. Soon, a few would venture out for a walk, enjoying the quiet. Some might even attempt to go shopping in the busy downtown district. The weekdays were usually better for the actual Carmel residents. When most of the tourists had gone, it seemed as if the residents almost owned their town again.

Aviva and Gladys enjoyed a wonderful morning, peeking in and out of the varied, well-stocked shops. More often than not, they both clucked their tongues at the outrageous prices the shops were now charging. There really weren't many good bargains left in the city, now that the shopkeepers had begun to take advantage of residents and tourists alike. Since the tourists kept pouring in and paying the prices, there was really never any need to discount. It was the one thing Aviva missed about L.A.—the great bargains in the wholesale district.

Aviva had found a wonderful Lalique cream and sugar set in the China Art Center, and Mrs. Barber had stopped into the Irish Linen shop and purchased a set of beautiful white linen napkins that she promptly presented to Aviva as an inn-warming present even though the inn was no longer new.

When Aviva protested that the gift was far too expensive, Gladys simply turned a deaf ear and strode on, ignoring I. Magnin and proceeding on down the street to the specialty stores. The inn-warming presents had become more and more frequent, and Aviva always tried to turn them down. But finally, realizing that it gave Gladys great pleasure to give her things, Aviva offered her protests only as a mere formality.

Although they were enjoying themselves, they both thought it a shame that Carmel-by-the-Sea had become so commercial. Aviva wished she had been around for the fight of 1916 when the residents of the little hamlet held out against the horrible idea of paved streets and electricity after the town had been incorporated. She would have given the local government resistance.

But she was always torn between the sublime and the practical. She did love the shops that were packed into the quaint buildings on Dolores Street. You could get anything you wanted in Carmel for a price. The only thing she really objected to was the plethora of T-shirt shops. It was a terrible fashion, one she hoped Jenny would never succumb to.

Lunch was a quiet meal at one of the little tearooms that had become so popular, and they sat enjoying the delicate little crustless sandwiches amid antiques and forest-green tablecloths enlivened by apricot-colored napkins. As they sipped their tea waiting for the check, Gladys pounced once again on the subject of Jeremy.

Since that night in Aviva's room, Gladys had felt that she could freely discuss the topic, woman to woman, with Aviva anytime she liked. Normally, that didn't bother Aviva. In fact, it was nice to have someone to confide in, and Gladys had never tried to sway her one way or another after she had said her piece that first evening.

"So, how is Jeremy?" Gladys demanded, raising the dainty teacup to her lips, her eyes searching over the rim.

"Just fine. Last time I talked to him he sent his love to you. But then, I think you already know that," Aviva gently reminded her.

"Of course I do, of course," Gladys retorted. "Such a gentleman; never forgets an old lady even when he's after a young one." Aviva smiled weakly. This was going to be another long discussion, she feared and, for some reason, she really didn't feel up to it that day. Shopping had been so pleasant and it was the first time in weeks that she had truly banished Jeremy's specter from her mind for longer than an hour. Surprisingly, though, Gladys dropped the subject.

"I've still got to stop and see Mr. Corbet before we go, Aviva," Gladys said as she pushed the small luncheon plate away from her and finished her last sip of tea.

"He's such a nice man. Do tell him hello for me, will you?" Aviva brightened at the change of subject.

"Don't you want to come with me?" It was almost

a command rather than a question, and Aviva demurred gently.

"No, I thought I'd go and see the contractor about the doors. They're still not working right. And I want to pick up something for Jenny. Would you like me to drive you or will you walk?"

"No need. I'll walk. It's only down Sixth Street. Why don't we meet at the car in forty-five minutes."

Although she did not admit it to herself, Aviva was happy to be free of Gladys's company for a while. She was beginning to be a constant reminder of Aviva's concern about Jeremy and the need to resolve the situation. Her step quickened when she realized she had only a short time to herself. Gladys's discussions with Mr. Corbet never lasted long, and Aviva would rather spend her time picking out something nice for Jenny than talking to a contractor.

Unfortunately, her visit to the carpentry shop dampened her spirits. The man was peeved that she wanted him to come back and cut down the doors again. She explained that she had waited so long to make her request because the doors hadn't swelled until the heavy fog set in, and then time had simply gotten away. Grumbling, he finally consented to come to adjust them the following day.

Attempting to revive her good humor, Aviva headed for the small group of shops known as La Rambla, sure that she would find something for Jenny in one of the antique stores there and maybe even have a moment to sit in the courtyard.

The time flew by, and after she had finally decided upon a china-faced doll dressed in a christening gown reminiscent of the early 1800s, Aviva stopped to rest in the little square and watch the other shoppers before she went to meet Gladys.

She had only just settled down on the little wrought-iron bench under the cypress tree when she heard her name called. Turning to look about the shops, she saw Tim emerge from the one and only T-shirt establishment that was ensconced in the pretty little shopping center.

"Hi," she said, trying to hide her disappointment as he sat down to join her. "What have you been up to?"

"I saw this a few days ago and decided to add it to my collection. How do you like it?" he asked, whipping a T-shirt out of the bag. Emblazoned on the front was the message "I love Carmel" the "love" a heart, not a word. Aviva gulped back her immediate reaction and just smiled.

"You still coming tonight? Sue told me she was going to work all day, so you should be free, right?" Tim went on, oblivious to the fact that she hadn't answered his previous question. Aviva glanced at Tim just long enough to take in the hopeful look in his eyes. So he still hadn't given up. He hid it well but his feeling for her was still there.

She really didn't feel like going to the party, but she had promised so long ago that she knew she couldn't back out now. Besides, it might be just the thing to help her make her decision about Jeremy. She had given Carmel a chance to be everything she wanted except a social haven. If she started going out with the younger people of the town, started opening up a little bit, living like a young woman, maybe then she wouldn't have those cravings to go running to Jeremy to fulfill those now-insistent needs in her.

"Of course I'm going. Where did you say it was?" she asked, ashamed that she had forgotten.

"You know Ian—the jeweler over on Torres Street? Well, he's celebrating. He just got a lease on a shop on Dolores and his business is bound to take off. But the party is still at the house behind the shop on Torres."

"Sounds good. I know exactly where it is but I'll be a little late. I want to make sure the house is settled down and Jenny is in bed before I come," Aviva said as she smiled at Tim. The pleasure her assurance gave him was evident, and Aviva decided that she definitely had been hiding too much since she moved to Carmel. Yes, a party would shed new light on things. She was sure Gladys wouldn't mind checking on Jenny.

"Are you sure you don't want me to come and get you? It wouldn't be any trouble," Tim asked quickly.

"No." She hesitated. "That's all right. I'll drive to town and meet you there." Cautious as usual, Aviva knew that she wanted to have her own transportation with her just in case the evening didn't turn out to be a total success. She wanted to be able to get home under her own power.

"Okay. See you tonight," Tim said, rising to go. Then, a second thought turned him around to face her again, "Heard from Jeremy lately?"

The question took Aviva aback. While Tim had not shown any outward sign of resentment, she was sure it hovered close to the surface and she knew she should choose her answer carefully.

"Oh, yes. He called a few days ago." Aviva cringed at her little white lie but for some reason she didn't want Tim to know how often she heard from Jeremy, fearing it might once again drive a wedge into their friendship as it almost had when Jeremy first appeared. "He said to give you his best."

"Yeah?" Tim seemed a bit incredulous but allowed the comment to pass lightly. "Well, give him mine, too. See you."

After Tim's long, lanky form had disappeared onto the crowded avenue, Aviva glanced at her watch and noticed that the time she had carved out for herself was gone. With a sigh she gathered her packages and headed off to meet Gladys. They met on the street and made their way casually back to the car.

When Aviva asked the woman to watch Jenny that evening Gladys consented without hesitation, but there was a note of disapproval in her voice when she commented on Aviva's plans. Aviva was surprised; she thought Gladys liked Tim. But maybe she saw him as some kind of obstacle in the way of Jeremy's advances, and Aviva was sure that Gladys's affection rested with the raven-haired man from Los Angeles. Shrugging once they got in the car and headed home, Aviva dismissed any uneasiness Gladys's comment had caused and turned her mind to Jenny's reaction to the doll. As Aviva expected, Jenny was delighted.

Sue had prepared a sumptuous meal for all the guests in honor of Mr. and Mrs. Jenkins's anniversary. Even Gladys seemed back to normal as Jenny dragged her into the living room to look at the pictures she had been working on all afternoon.

By eight o'clock Aviva felt reasonably certain that she could sneak away from the group around the hearth.

As she said her good-evenings, she came to the Jenkinses. Martha and Bill were an unusual pair but obviously well suited to each other. He was a dapper little man, dressed to kill. His small frame was covered from head to toe in forest green, including his patent shoes. His dull gray hair was styled, not cut, and Aviva could just imagine the problems this little man caused when he walked in to have his hair done... probably by some buxom wench.

Martha was portly, making Aviva think of Jack Sprat and his wife. She looked extremely down-to-earth and Aviva guessed that she had run their home with an iron hand during the past fifty years. They were charming, and she enjoyed the way Martha quietly but firmly controlled Bill when his jokes became a little risqué.

Both expressed their delight with the extras the inn had provided for their very special celebration, and Aviva blushed at the compliments. She was reluctantly thinking of leaving when Sue came in to offer more coffee. Aviva lifted her eyebrows in surprise when she saw the girl. Sue had changed for the evening and was dressed in a simple brown shirtwaist dress and pumps, so different from her usual jeans and sweater. She looked quite the lady and Aviva decided to offer her permanent employment the next day, even though she knew she could not offer top salary right away.

With one last good-bye she left the house and drove the short distance into town. Finding the jewelry shop easily enough, given the number of cars parked in front, Aviva pulled up and stopped. She adjusted her shawl as she walked up the short gravel path and knocked at the door. From inside she could hear the strains of music reminiscent of the sixties. It had not really occurred to her to think about what this party would be like. When the door opened, her heart sank as she stared at the young, frizzy-haired woman before her.

Aviva felt as if she had walked into a time warp. Old and young were dressed alike—hippies who had never realized that the seventies had already come and gone. Love beads abounded and Aviva somehow felt like the Queen of Sheba who suddenly realized that there were other people living outside her castle walls.

Smiling bravely, she said hello to the few people she knew as she walked through the tiny shop searching for Tim. He was a bit hard to find. In the dim light everyone looked alike. For the most part the men were bearded and mustachioed, all with longer hair than was fashionable, and most were clad in T-shirts and jeans.

Then she spotted him, standing by a jumble of wine bottles and beer cans. Smiling, she went to greet him. He looked as perfect in his "I Love Carmel" T-shirt as Aviva looked out of place in her finery. Determined not to let her embarrassment over her dress ruin the evening, she put on a bright, brave smile. In the back of her mind, though, she was comparing every man there to Jeremy, whose clean-cut appearance was more to her liking.

"Hi. I thought you said this party started at seven. It's only a little past nine now and it looks like everyone's been here all day." She congratulated herself on her bright tone, and her own bravado allowed her to relax a bit.

"Most of them have. You know how artists are: work hard, play hard." She wasn't sure if Tim was all that happy to see her. Maybe he was just a little surprised at what she was wearing—a chic, black silk ensemble. She should have asked what people would be wearing.

"Want a drink?" Tim asked suddenly, looking at her through bleary eyes.

"Sure," she said, realizing that he had already had just a little too much wine. "Here, let me do that." She took the jug of wine from him gently. His spillage had already spread across the Formica counter and was splashing onto the worn floor.

"Thanks. I guess I've been here longer than I thought," he confessed, shrugging his shoulders with little regret.

"Tim." Two people had moved toward them and now stood so close that Aviva felt confined, as if the world were moving in on her. Aviva was aware of the smell of marijuana in the room and clenched her teeth when the taller, scruffier of the two men held out a twisted cigarette to Tim. Aviva lowered her eyes, watching as Tim nodded his refusal. Then the cigarette was thrust under her nose. "You, madam?"

"No, thank you," Aviva said, trying to smile

though her heart wasn't in it. Luckily the man only shrugged and put the cigarette to his own lips.

"So, man," the shorter man spoke, his voice lazy. Aviva looked askance at him. His clothes were not old but it seemed as if they hadn't been washed in weeks, and in his ear he sported a small gold hoop earring. "What's going on?"

"Not much," Tim's words were slurred and he leaned back against the counter. "I got a commission. It's hard work, but I think I can really make a statement with it."

"No kidding. That's a new one," the short man said. "I'm so busy doing what everyone else wants just to pay the rent I haven't been able to think about the message. But I'm going to start working on my monolith any day now."

"What do you do?" Aviva asked, trying to fit into the conversation gracefully. The man looked at her as if she were crazy.

"Cort does sculpture," Tim interjected. "Big stuff. Like when a city wants something for the front of a library." He seemed incredulous that she hadn't recognized the sculptor.

"Oh," she said, "I haven't been here too long. I'm sorry I didn't recognize you." She could have kicked herself. She shouldn't be apologizing. Half the world didn't know who the man was!

"That's okay. But it won't take you long to figure out who's who around here, right, Tim?" The taller man nodded his assent and Tim simply took a sip of wine. Aviva looked at the threesome and wondered if, indeed, she would ever want to get to know them.

"I'm sure you're right," she said sweetly. "But if you'll excuse me, I think I'm going to mingle a bit." With that she made her escape, breathing a sigh of relief that she was not going to have to pay homage to the little man that evening.

Moving about the small house, Aviva noted that everyone seemed to be having a great time. And after a while, things even started looking up for her. She had congratulated the jeweler on his lease and spent an interesting half hour with a young woman sculptor who had just recently joined the artistic community. Still, though, Aviva felt strange, as out of place among these philosophically inclined, insular people who lived to create lasting works of art as she had been with the glittering shakers and movers of L.A.

Finally the rush of the day took its toll, along with the poor wine. Aviva's head felt light and there was the beginning of a headache lurking at the base of her skull. She really would have preferred to be at home. The party was interesting, though it was not exactly the panacea for her troubled mind that she had hoped it would be.

Looking around for Tim, she found him in the middle of the most rowdy group. She decided to slip quietly out the back door for some air before saying her good-byes and thank-yous.

The little fenced-in garden was terribly overgrown. Untying her shawl she draped it over both shoulders as she carefully picked her way across the ground to the white picket fence. The night was gorgeous, clear and brisk—a perfect evening.

She found herself pitying the people in Los Angeles

who could never see the stars because of the glare of city lights. They rarely felt the coolness of early spring.

"What're you doing out here?" It was Tim; his slurred speech had startled her.

"Just getting a breath of air. Are you okay?" Aviva asked, squinting at him through the darkness.

"Couldn't be any better, my dear." His W. C. Fields imitation was terrible. He fell, rather than leaned back, against the fence, and Aviva put out her hand to steady him, afraid he might hurt himself.

"No need to worry, pretty lady. You havin' a good time?" She nodded, thinking it better than telling him the truth. Aviva had never seen him act like this. She didn't even know he drank anything but beer and an occasional brandy.

"Good, 'cause it's going to get even better." With that he drew himself up, towering over her. As he took a deep breath Aviva was taken aback by the sour smell of wine and smoke.

So, he had been indulging, she thought to herself. Before she had time to berate him she was engulfed in his long arms. His face came down awkwardly on hers, his lips searching her face. Aviva struggled, attempting to free herself without causing a scene.

"Tim, what are you doing?" she hissed at him once her mouth was free. "You're drunk."

"Am not. Love you, Aviva." He was not even listening to her, and as his arms tightened their hold she began to panic. His arms were stronger than she would ever have imagined. The delicate-looking windows he worked on were heavy when they were finished, and the many years of installing them had made Tim's hold viselike. Then as she realized who it was that had entrapped her, Aviva's panic subsided. She would have to talk her way out of this.

"Tim." Her voice was calm and strong. "You've got to stop this. It isn't like you."

He relaxed his hold, looked at her for an instant as he tried to comprehend what she was saying. For a moment it seemed as if the wine had a stronger effect on him than she had. He wavered, trying to decide whether to resume his unwanted advances or back off and leave her, as he always did when she asked him to.

Aviva stood still, waiting for him to relax further. The moment she felt his hands slip to her waist she seized her moment, reached behind her, grabbed his wrists and gently moved them away from her body. Holding them tightly she lowered herself onto the wet unruly grass, urging Tim to follow.

"Tim," she said quietly as soon as they were seated, "Tim." His head hung down on his chest and she wondered if he had gone to sleep. How funny that would have been. One word and a man who was ready to take her under the stars of Carmel was discouraged enough to simply fall asleep. But he was awake, and he raised his pale face to hers.

"You wouldn't have said no if it had been Jeremy," Tim complained in a small voice.

"You're wrong, Tim. I would have if he was drunk, as you are."

"Really?" he asked, his smile lopsided, his eyes half closed.

"Yes," Aviva reiterated, trying not to smile. Tim could be dense sometimes. It didn't matter that her explanation had to do with drunkenness rather than who it was that was attacking her. But it seemed that the message was lost on him.

"I want you to love me like I love you." His eyes had taken on that sad look of a man who is easily controlled, and Aviva's heart went out to him.

"No, Tim. That can never be," she answered with finality, releasing his wrists as she did so. The silence seemed interminable as his head bobbed about his shoulders. She doubted whether he was thinking much of anything. More than likely his declaration of love was the last one she would hear from him. He would be too embarrassed ever to bring it up again.

Finally he spoke. "Okay, okay." Rising unsteadily, he stood for a minute above her and she held her breath, afraid that he might try to reach down and embrace her again. But Tim simply shook his head and staggered away to rejoin the party.

Alone, Aviva let out a sigh of relief, raising her eyes to the bright night sky. Her eyes moved about, lighting on star after star. Slowly a smile spread across her face. It was a sweet, knowing smile, one that brought a glisten to her eyes, a happy blush to her face. Thanks to Tim, thanks to the party, thanks to learning that she would never find what she was looking for as a woman there in Carmel, her decision had been made.

At that moment Aviva knew that she would soon be with Jeremy. To hell with deadlines and risks.

Chapter Seven

The drive home seemed interminable. Aviva could have sworn that she passed the same intersection three times before finally finding the last tree-lined stretch of road that would take her to the inn, a telephone and Jeremy's voice.

Everything seemed so clear now. Just because she wanted a simpler life didn't mean that she had to adapt to every nuance of the place in which she lived. Aviva had truly enjoyed some aspects of the party. A few of the people she had spoken with had been interesting, making her wish that she had some sort of artistic talent. The woman sculptor, the poet, even Ian the jeweler all had intrigued her with knowledge of the arts.

Yes, it had been enjoyable. But now, away from it all, she could see that it was a world in which she could walk but not live. While she could appreciate the work all those people represented, she could never convince them, or herself, that it interested her enough to make the arts the focal point of her existence. She was a person who needed smaller, less cerebral centers of gravity. Aviva wanted a home, a family, a few good friends whom she could count on. But most of all she wanted Jeremy to be a part of that secure, intimate little world.

She had been so blind, burying herself in Whaler's Inn. She loved it. It was the core of the universe for her and it housed the most precious thing in her life—Jenny. But even a universe as small as the inn could expand enough to let just one more person in, one more being to love, to cherish.

The tires scraped the graveled drive and Aviva was finally home. For a moment she simply sat in the black night, the motor idling, her heart racing. Mixed with her excitement were the ragged edges of her hesitations regarding Jeremy. Determined, though, to call him before her courage waned and the fabric of her apprehensions wove itself back together, she turned off the ignition, opened the door and moved quickly toward the back door of the house.

Fumbling with her keys she finally found the right one and let herself in as quietly as she could. Before she could turn on the light Cherry was at her feet nuzzling her shoes to make sure it was she. Reaching down she groped for his long silky ears and, finding them, rubbed them as she bent down and whispered to her silent friend.

"This is it, Cherry. I'm going to take the plunge, so wish me luck. I hope I'm right about this whole thing, so keep your paws crossed!" Planting a light kiss on his cold wet nose she led him back to his blanket by the stove and headed toward the telephone in the alcove. In the closeness of the little nook and the safety

of the dark, her long, tapered fingers shook as she felt
for the numbers and dialed directory assistance in Los
Angeles.

"Operator, a listing for Jeremy Crowley...Beverly
Hills, I believe."

"That listing is in Santa Monica: 555-7941," came
the clipped voice over the line.

"Thank you, operator," Aviva breathed into the
phone, not trusting her mind to remember the number if she spoke too loudly. After three abortive tries
at dialing the number, it finally occurred to her to
reach up for the light pull. The little room was illuminated with a soft glow and she blinked, her eyes taking a moment to adjust. Dialing again, she then
reached up and pulled the cord, once more envelop-
ing herself in darkness. It seemed right somehow that
she should be talking to Jeremy encased in such intimate nonlight.

One, two, three rings. The phone rang and rang
again, Aviva's heart racing faster each time she heard
the tone. What if he wasn't there? It was so late she
couldn't imagine that he wouldn't be home. Or worse
yet, what if someone was with him? After all, he had
no commitment to her, not really.

Aviva's heart rebelled at the thought. But he does,
the little voice in the back of her mind screamed. He
had said he loved her. He had sent her flowers and
letters, made phone calls. Damn it—he did have a
commitment and he was going to honor it if it killed
him. After all, it was Jeremy who was responsible for
this step she was taking. It was Jeremy who had en-

ticed her to uproot her life once again, take a chance. Then, she heard it. The receiver clicked.

"Hello?" His voice was deep and low and sweet. Was it tinged with sleep? Husky after a night of loving someone else? She couldn't tell. Aviva couldn't speak; her nerves were raw, her mind racing on to what might be happening there in his apartment rather than concentrating on what she wanted to do at that very moment. Taking a deep breath she finally answered.

"Jeremy?" Her voice sounded so loud, almost echoing off the three little walls of the alcove. Clearing her throat she tried again, this time modulating her tone, attempting to calm the catch of nervousness.

"Jeremy? It's Aviva."

Silence greeted the admission. A deep, warm sigh could be heard on the other end of the phone and then he spoke. "Aviva. My love," he said, and she could almost see the soft, sweet smile playing about his lips as he relaxed, cradling the receiver even closer as if it would also bring her closer to him. Aviva smiled, too. How stupid she had been to create situations out of nothing. There was no way he would have greeted her in such a manner if anyone else had been in his apartment.

"I have waited so long for you to make this call. I love you. Please tell me that this means what I think it does." Aviva's heart leaped, then settled in her breast. He wanted her. He truly did.

"I think it does," she admitted shyly.

"Don't think, darling. Don't let one little nagging, ugly thought enter that beautiful head of yours. Just do what you have decided to do. What you knew had to happen. Come to me." His command was gentle, and Aviva's mind reached out for his strength.

"I will, Jeremy, but I am scared," Aviva whispered into the phone, holding it with both hands as if at any moment it might simply fade, disappear, and she would be alone. It was as if she were holding a tenuous lifeline. Holding, but afraid to reel herself in until she was sure that it would hold her heavy weight—the weight of suspicion and sadness she had carried for so long now.

Even now, though, as she spoke to Jeremy, the weight seemed to be lifting, dissipating. Soon she hoped she would be able to lose herself completely in the safety of Jeremy. Oh, how she hoped, wanted, demanded that he wouldn't let her down.

"I know. Really, I do. Trust me." A small gasp escaped her lips. Trust—how she wanted to trust him. But he would not even give her time to consider whether she should, he spoke again so quickly. "When are you coming?"

"Well, I hadn't really thought about it. I just decided a little while ago and—" Who was she kidding? Certainly not herself. She would have left that instant if she possibly could have, left immediately so that her personal demons wouldn't know where she had gone, wouldn't have been able to follow her in their confusion.

"I think tomorrow, if that's all right. Tomorrow,

yes." Her words were falling on top of one another, over one another; her heart was soaring.

"Of course it's all right. Just let me know what time. Now, I'm going to give you my office number. Do you have a pencil?" he asked. Now the excitement in his voice was evident, too, and Aviva wondered if Jeremy could possibly be as nervous as she.

"Yes... I mean no. Not right here. But wait. I'll get one from the desk. Just hold on a minute." Aviva put the phone down and rushed off as quietly as she could to rummage through her desk drawer.

"I've got it," she said breathlessly, retrieving the receiver. "Oh—but Jeremy, I've forgotten to get some paper!" Aviva berated herself. How could she be so stupid? It was as if she had forgotten how to do the most simple tasks now that she had actually committed herself to this visit. Jeremy's deep, delighted chuckle seemed to calm her and she once again sat down and leaned back against the wall, laughing quietly with him. "I hope this isn't a bad omen."

"No, it's a wonderful omen. It means you're just as excited as I am about this trip." He consoled her, enjoying her obvious nervousness. "There is a much easier way, you know, and if you hadn't run off so quickly I could have saved you a trip to the desk."

"I'm sorry. I don't know what's gotten into me," she said, feeling suddenly shy. She knew she was acting like a child trying so hard to please that it was almost comical.

"I think you do, Aviva Thompson, I think you do," he answered, and Aviva mentally had to agree with him. Of course she knew; she just didn't want to admit it out loud yet. When she didn't say anything in response he continued, "Anyway, Gladys has the number."

"Gladys!" Aviva retorted, knowing that the information really shouldn't have surprised her.

"Yes, Gladys. Now don't get upset. I hadn't asked her to spy on you. I gave her my number because she had asked for some advice and I wanted her to be able to call me if she felt the need," Jeremy gently reprimanded her.

"I'm not upset and I didn't think you had asked her to spy on me," Aviva defended herself. So he had noticed the tension between Gladys and her. Well, luckily, that was all behind her now. For a moment she wondered how she could ever have thought that Gladys was anything but a well-intentioned old woman who needed to be loved and wanted just like anyone else.

"I'm glad that you gave Gladys your number. I hope she took advantage of it and called you once in a while. She certainly must have been lonely around here those first few weeks."

"Does that mean there has been a change in temperature between you and her?" Jeremy asked, the note of surprise and pleasure scarcely hidden.

"You might say that," Aviva admitted. "She really is a dear and I am sorry that I was so cool to her in the beginning."

"Aviva, you are full of surprises tonight. Now, call me at the office the moment you know when you'll be here. Are you driving or flying?"

"Flying, I think. I don't want to waste one more minute than is absolutely necessary," she confessed. "And, Jeremy..."

"Yes?"

"I...I love you."

"Oh, I hope so. See you soon, Aviva." Aviva murmured her good-byes and listened as he hung up the phone. For a long while she simply sat there in the dark, listening to the dial tone, thinking of nothing in particular except that the sound of his voice was the one and only thing she had wanted only moments earlier and now that she had heard it there was nothing more in the world she could want.

Replacing the receiver, she finally rose and left the alcove and climbed the stairs, rubbing her eyes as she went. She was exhausted but it was the kind of tiredness that she knew she would never be unhappy to experience. It was all-encompassing, warm and settling. Aviva knew she would sleep well that night because it was a sure bet that the next would not be passed dreaming.

The following morning was so hectic Aviva wondered if she would make her flight at all. Jenny wanted to go with her. Not because she was afraid of Aviva's leaving but because she wanted to see Jeremy so much. Gladys, trying to arrange the flight, kept calling out every three minutes to find out if Aviva wanted a special meal or seat. Sue, thankfully, accepted a full-time position with the inn and was going to start immediately, staying over while Aviva was away. Finally, she had stolen a moment to call Jeremy, and the sound of his voice staved off the nasty little doubts that had begun to rise in her mind. The sound of him was all she needed to reassure her that this trip was not folly, that she needed to find out once and for all if they could make their relationship work.

Aviva had risen early and made out the bills that would be coming due in the week she was away, writing thank-you notes ahead of time and leaving instructions for Sue to mail them out at the proper intervals. It would be awful if someone received a thank-you note postmarked before the visitor had actually left the inn.

Finally she was packed, all instructions were given, Jenny was kissed and Cherry petted, and a cab was waiting to take her to the small airport where she would catch a twin-engine plane to the Santa Monica airport. With a determined step she entered the cab, waved and was gone, instinctively crossing her fingers in a childish gesture to ensure that this risk would pay off.

The flight had been ludicrous, it was so short. By the time the little plane reached cruising altitude it was time to begin the descent into the Santa Monica airport. As she watched, Aviva could see the grand Los Angeles International airport just below her, the vast expanse of the San Fernando Valley, the Hollywood Hills, the glittering Pacific Ocean and the high rises of downtown Los Angeles.

Aviva had wondered if there was another city in the world that could overwhelm its suburbs and surroundings the way Los Angeles did. People never said they were going to Santa Monica or Torrance or Long

Beach. They simply said they were headed for L.A. Looking at it from the window of the little plane, Aviva had suddenly felt as if she didn't want to land—she simply wanted to turn around and go home. It was so immense, so sprawling, so impersonal, yet holding such personal memories. What was she doing there?

"Are you all right?" The young man in the seat next to her had lightly touched her arm, startling her out of her nagging concerns about her journey.

"Certainly I am," she had stuttered, looking into his young blue eyes. "It's just that ... I'm a little nervous about this small plane." The excuse seemed feasible and the boy had turned away after apologizing for disturbing her.

But Aviva realized then that her nervousness regarding the situation must be terribly evident if a mere stranger could see it. Knowing then that she must compose herself before they landed and she had to face Jeremy, Aviva opened her purse and took out her compact. She couldn't see what the boy next to her had seen. According to her reflection she looked as she always did: her hair fresh and clean, pulled back softly from her face; her makeup understated. Only her eyes looked guarded, perhaps even a bit frantic. Smoothing her pale blue skirt over her knees, Aviva had fastened her seat belt, leaned her head back and waited for the plane to touch ground.

Now she stood in the small terminal, alone, her heart pounding like thunder as her eyes searched each face that passed, looking for Jeremy's black eyes to meet hers. But he wasn't there. She couldn't believe it. He had not come to meet the plane after all, and he had promised that he wouldn't be late. Suddenly Aviva felt a tap on her shoulder and whirled around; the ecstatic smile on her face faded the instant she saw that it was not Jeremy who had summoned her.

"Aviva Thompson?" the young black woman queried.

"Yes?" Aviva answered, confused but hoping that she brought some message from Jeremy.

"I'm Kelly Cortland," she said brightly, waiting as if she expected some kind of greeting. Receiving none she realized that Aviva had no idea who she was and quickly hurried on to assuage the other woman's evident concern. "Mr. Crowley's secretary. I'm sorry; I just assumed that you would know who I was."

"Is something wrong? Has something happened to Jeremy?" Relief that someone had rescued her from what seemed like a foreign land mingled with concerned curiosity, and Aviva instinctively reached out and took the other woman's arm.

"No." Kelly laughed. "Nothing has happened except the usual. He sends his apologies and his regrets. Unfortunately, one of his biggest clients stopped in unexpectedly and wanted to go over some questions he had regarding a new building Jeremy is developing for him. He said he would see you tonight and that I was to take you anywhere you wanted, deliver you back to his house, and he would meet you there as soon as he could. Oh, and these are for you with his love." Her lips parted in a wide smile as she handed Aviva a bunch of lavender. "He said to tell you that these were awfully hard to find but that you would know what he meant by them." Kelly said this proudly, obviously totally enthralled by her boss's romantic intentions.

"Thank you," Aviva answered, taking the flowers. She did remember the last time she and Jeremy had seen lavender together—the morning Jenny had had an intimate breakfast with him in his room.

Smiling weakly, still confused by the turn of events, Aviva didn't have time to sort out her feelings as Kelly steered her toward the baggage claim and out the door to her waiting car. A fleeting thought, though, had caught hold of her mind and would not let go. Shouldn't Jeremy have dropped everything in order to meet her at the airport? He had known she was coming, and she was sure that had he explained to his client, they could have put off their meeting until another day. But once settled in Kelly's little economy car, she had no time to consider it any further as the girl kept up her running commentary on Jeremy, the business and her pleasure that Aviva had come to visit.

"He just never stopped talking about your beautiful inn and you and your daughter," Kelly was saying as they made their way down Santa Monica Boulevard. "I don't think I have ever seen him happier or more rested. Of course, your place must look crazy by now with all those flowers."

"How did you know about that?" Aviva was suddenly alert and she turned in her seat to look at the young woman beside her. The question was caustic but Aviva felt she had the right to demand an answer. How dare Jeremy discuss their personal business with anyone? It was great he enjoyed the inn but did he have to tell his secretary about her, the family and his courtship procedures?

Kelly looked startled at the harshness of Aviva's tone and cocked her head slightly, her smile and chatter disappearing simultaneously.

"I—" She started to speak, then stopped abruptly. Considering how to address Aviva seemed to be a problem and she hesitated, but only for a minute.

"I ordered them for you, Mrs. Thompson. You see, Mr. Crowley wanted something very special and trusted me to go to the florist to pick out the flowers. I hope that doesn't upset you. You see, he thinks very highly of you."

Kelly finished her speech and stared straight ahead in silence as she drove. Tension filled the interior of the car. Aviva felt like an idiot. Her blush of embarrassment would have told the whole story if Kelly had only looked her way. But since she didn't, Aviva knew she would have to apologize verbally.

"Kelly, I'm sorry. I don't know what got into me. I had no right to speak to you so harshly," Aviva began, trying to make amends. "I guess I'm a little jumpy. I used to live here, and coming back is just a bit hard. And, of course, I am disappointed that Jeremy wasn't at the airport." Aviva knew her explanation sounded childish but it was all she could come up with; her mortification was too great for her to attempt anything more rational.

"It's okay. I'd be disappointed, too, if I were you." Kelly shrugged, accepting the apology but definitely cooling toward her passenger.

"Kelly, I really am sorry. Can I make it up to you over lunch? I know it's kind of late, but I haven't eaten today and I would appreciate it if you'd join me." Aviva really had no intention to alienate Kelly, who she knew was not responsible for Aviva's disappointment.

"Sure, Mrs. Thompson. I'd like that," Kelly said, once again flashing her dazzling smile. Soon she was chattering on as if nothing had happened, asking Aviva's preference in food.

"Well, I hate to admit this, and it may be out of our way, but there's a small hamburger stand on Vine Street between Sunset and Hollywood boulevards. It's called Molly's, and I've been dying for one of their hamburgers for ages." Aviva bit her lip, wondering what Kelly would think of her now. Perhaps she should have suggested Moustache Café or St. Germain but the thought of a Molly's hamburger was driving her wild.

Luckily, Kelly thought it was a fabulous idea and headed toward Hollywood to find the little stand. They sat there for almost two hours, each of them indulging in a second burger while the Oriental woman behind the counter watched in wonder. The smoke from the open grill blew about them, and Aviva closed her eyes remembering all the bright, sunny days she had sat there with Sam, discussing his business when it was just getting off the ground.

Oh, she thought wistfully, *Jeremy was right. There had been some wonderful times. What a shame that they were so few and far between.*

By the time they left and headed toward Jeremy's

home in Santa Monica, Aviva was once again becoming nervous. The hustle and bustle of Hollywood was too much to take all at once. She hadn't seen so many people rushing about the streets since she had left L.A. But the nervousness caused by the activity on the street was nothing compared to what Aviva felt when Kelly pulled up in front of a small Spanish-style bungalow and parked the car.

This was Jeremy's house. This was where she was going to stay for the next week. This was the house in which she would get to know Jeremy Crowley on his own terms on his own turf, and the thought brought a terrible pounding to Aviva's temples.

Jeremy was not there when the women entered through the front door. The house was quiet and neat as a pin, giving Aviva hope that the next week would prove to be exactly what she had hoped for. The walls were white, the furniture sleek but comfortable, and the art work subtle yet sophisticated.

"Shall I leave these here?" Kelly interrupted Aviva's curious examination of the front room and Aviva turned to look at the girl, who indicated the luggage at her feet.

"Yes," Aviva answered, feeling somewhat embarrassed to ask Kelly to help her put them in Jeremy's bedroom. She knew her concerns were stupid and old-fashioned, but she nevertheless didn't want Kelly to think ill of her. Besides, she wasn't even sure herself that she would be staying in Jeremy's room. Maybe they should take things slowly. She probably should stay in the guest room, if there was one, until they had time to get used to each other again.

"I'll take them out of here later. Right now I think I'll just acclimate myself to my new surroundings if that's okay with you."

"Okay," Kelly answered. "Do you want some company until Mr. Crowley gets here or—"

"No, of course not. I know it's only four-thirty but I'll bet you could use an extra half hour to yourself, so why don't you go on home."

"Oh, thanks, Mrs. Thompson. I really appreciate it. It's always nice to get off a little early even if all you've been doing is having fun all day."

With more than a little relief Aviva let Kelly out the front door, thanked her and waved good-bye before turning back to investigate the house a bit further.

Within the hour Aviva was feeling extremely at ease. The house had held no surprises. The kitchen was well stocked and she wondered if that was for her benefit or if he really did cook for himself. Given his performance at the inn with breakfast, Aviva imagined that he actually did manage to do very well by himself in the kitchen on a daily basis.

There was a den, neatly "cluttered" with the tools of his craft and a pair of very worn slippers. There was a small guest room that was almost Spartan in its decoration. Obviously it was not used very often or Jeremy would have decorated it with the same care as he had taken with the other rooms of the house. It was there, though, that she was greeted with a small surprise.

Beside the bed stood a vase of yellow roses. Aviva could not resist walking to them and burying her nose in the velvety buds. Her eye caught sight of a card with her name on it and Aviva immediately opened it.

Inside was another of Jeremy's short messages that carried so much meaning. It read simply "Just in Case." So, she thought, she was not the only one who had wondered about the sleeping arrangements. The idea that Jeremy must be as nervous as she made her chuckle, and she found she couldn't wait for him to get home.

Finally Aviva made her way around the house and stood in front of the last door. Opening it, she found herself in his bedroom. Suddenly he was there, surrounding her, penetrating her. His scent was everywhere. The stability she had questioned was evident. On the bureau were pictures: small, large, vertical and horizontal. Each of them seemed to be of a family nature.

The woman Aviva thought to be his mother was beautiful: tall, sophisticated and foreign-looking—perhaps French. His father was no less handsome, but rather than being striking in a physical sense, the man in the picture seemed to exude an intellectual refinement, an attraction that could make itself felt even through the glass. There were old framed photographs that Aviva thought must be of grandparents, aunts and uncles.

Aviva walked around the room, running her hands lightly over the well-oiled antique furniture, opening the delicate French doors that led to a small garden. Unable to resist climbing into the bed when at last she stood beside it, she lay her head down, sinking into the down pillows underneath the spread, and slept.

Her dream was wonderful. Jeremy was kissing her, running his fingers through her hair, whispering that he loved her, until she knew that she could no longer stand such gentleness, no longer lie then under his sweet ministrations without returning his love, taking him in a way she had never imagined she could act toward a man.

Then her eyes were opened to a darkened room and in her half sleep she realized how warm she was, how comfortable she felt, how her dream was really no dream at all but reality.

Lying beside her was Jeremy, his lips tracing the hollow of her cheek and running down to her chin, where he lingered for a moment before raising his face and whispering to her.

"Wake up. I can't stand one more minute of your being unaware that I am here, loving you, wanting you. Wake up, my love." His words were insistent, drawing her carefully out of her deep sleep.

Through bleary eyes she looked up at him. His face was so close that even in the dark of the room she could make out his every feature. Dark eyes danced under his long, black lashes. His tanned skin seemed almost to shimmer with an iridescence all its own. His hair waved and bobbed over his forehead, and only a glint of his white, white teeth could be seen as he continued to speak to her, kiss her.

"What time is it?" she asked groggily, reaching up her hand unsteadily to brush his hair back from his broad brow.

"Eight o'clock," he answered, smiling down at her.

"So late?" Her tongue slipped out to moisten her lips. "Did you just get home?"

"Just this moment. I should have let you sleep but

I just couldn't. I wanted to apologize immediately for not picking you up today, for not being at your beck and call the moment your feet hit the ground." Once again his lips descended, this time meeting hers squarely. Gently, he rotated his mouth, attempting to match the exquisite contours of hers, covering hers entirely with his insistent kiss, forcing her out of her sleep and into the world they now shared.

It started slowly for her, deep in the pit of her stomach. The comfort of sleep was being replaced by the physical demands she could not ignore. The feeling spread, inching its way into every nerve, every inch of muscle, through the core of her very bones until the desire exploded in her mind and heart.

"I should take you to dinner," he said frantically in the millisecond between the time his lips left hers and came once again to rest in the tiny hollow under her ear.

"Yes, you should," she said, gasping, her breath coming short and fast.

"Are you hungry?" The question seemed ludicrous, given their present posture, but Aviva did not even think of how silly it was.

"No ... you?" She managed to breathe the words.

"Yes. Starving, my darling. Starving." The last word melted into her consciousness. Leaving no room for misunderstanding, Jeremy's actions corroborated his statement.

His hands moved to the small pearl buttons of her blouse and eased them out of the buttonholes one by one. His fingers lingered for a moment after each of them, darting under the silken fabric to touch her skin, still warm from her rest, to roam over the mound of each breast.

All vestiges of sleep now firmly put aside, Aviva responded in kind, pulling his shirt from his slacks and running her hands up his back, enjoying the feel of his smooth skin, cupping his ribs, struggling with the small buttons on his shirt.

Now there was no thought of right or wrong, of tomorrow or the day after. It felt so right being with him, loving him, enjoying all the things he was and would do to her body, tell her mind. If there could be danger, it certainly wasn't present. But Aviva would not let it be. She wouldn't let him be Sam.

The bed did not creak here in his little house as it had at the inn when he rolled over on top of her, both their chests bared now to the warm air. Aviva moved under him, compelling him to take her further to the outer reaches of ecstasy. Slipping from the rest of their clothes, wordlessly urgent, they finally lay naked, their bodies slick and shining, each heart matching the other's, beat for beat.

Aviva's eyes closed, trying to force her mind to slow down, to remember each and every touch. Remember his every groan of delight so that she might recall it again and again and do exactly the same the next time they touched, the next time they loved.

Quickly the end came, neither having the desire or the self-control to extend their delightful exercise. Jeremy called her name, raising his head to the ceiling, as if looking at her were too much to bear when their final coupling reached its height. Laying his head beside hers on the pillows, he continued to call her name until his words were no more than an echo in her mind and he had fallen asleep, his hand resting on the soft slope of her stomach.

For the longest time Aviva watched him breathing deeply beside her, her mind thinking of nothing more than how beautiful he appeared. Then, without thinking, she rose from the bed, wishing to look at him from another angle, wondering if by standing away she might be given a sign before she completely released herself to him. Perhaps if she stood by the French doors and looked at him carelessly flung on the bed he would appear more vulnerable, more human.

But all she saw was the man to whom she had given her heart, entrusted her well-being, her psyche. Like a cat she walked toward the bed and stared down at him, fighting the urge to reach out, rouse him once more, take him to her again and again. He was so tired, he needed to sleep, but the knowledge did not change the fact that she didn't want him to sleep.

Aviva wanted him with her, reassuring her, holding her against his virile body. Stooping, she picked up his discarded shirt and slipped into it, breathing deeply of his scent mingled with that of the heavy starch. She loved the crisp feeling of the collar against her neck, the coolness of the cotton as it fell over her breasts to just below her hips.

Her legs felt weak. Her entire body shivered from the wonderful exertion of their lovemaking. If only each night of her life could be spent with him this way. If only each of their days could be as they had been in Carmel.

Now, though, the thoughts came again, spreading

through her mind like milk spilled on a tabletop. Tomorrow, in the daylight, would it be the same when they ventured out to the streets and shops and restaurants where his friends were, his business acquaintances? Would she still know the man she had come to love or would he be different somehow? Subtly changed? His voice just a shade louder, his movements a tad quicker, his sweet demeanor perhaps a little more raucous, as it had been that first night they had met?

"Please," Aviva prayed, "please don't let tomorrow be disappointing. Keep him as he should be, as he was meant to be. For me. Please."

Looking down, she noticed their clothes, tangled and entwined together at her feet. She smiled as she realized that she could not even remember when they had shed the last of their garments, so anxious were they to be together. For no good reason she picked up each of their garments and folded them, placing them in a pile on the small chair by the highboy, never letting her eyes roam from the sleeping man on the bed. Then, carefully, she covered him with the blanket that lay at the foot of the bed, climbed in next to him and gently placed her arm over his broad shoulders.

Aviva was mesmerized by the movement of her arm as it kept time with his breathing. Up and down, so gently that it was almost imperceptible. Her fingers moved to touch the hard bone of his shoulder without waking him. It felt solid, safe and solid, just as she wanted him to be forever. How she wished he would wake up, if only long enough to kiss her one last time before she allowed sleep to overtake her.

Could this be, she wondered as she watched him, her final reward for all those years with Sam, all those years wondering about her father? For the past months when she was alone and afraid that her venture wouldn't work? Could Jeremy Crowley really be the one person who would make the rest of her life seem like a little bit of heaven? Watching him now, knowing that he was unaware of her thoughts, unaware of her warm body lying next to his, waiting for his touch, Aviva realized that she could wait. She had been patient so long, she could wait a few more hours until the light of morning.

Chapter Eight

"Yes, Gladys, I know I should have called yesterday when I got in but—" Aviva tried to get a word in edgeways but Gladys was intent on expressing her displeasure at the other woman's lack of thoughtfulness.

As she listened, Aviva sat back in the deep leather armchair and surveyed Jeremy's den, thinking all the while that she better get used to Gladys's mothering. It was actually nice to think that the old woman had been worried. But if she had been that worried she would have called Jeremy. More than likely she was just upset that Aviva hadn't bothered to fill her in immediately on how things were going.

"Gladys," Aviva tried once more to break in, this time successfully, "I had absolutely nothing to tell you yesterday even if I had called. Jeremy was caught up with business and I was so tired that I just fell asleep. When I woke up it was just too late to call."

Aviva smiled to herself. It certainly had been too late to call, given Jeremy's greeting when he arrived home. The last thing on her mind had been to call

Gladys and tell her that she and Jeremy had gotten along just fine.

"Well, I guess I can understand that," Gladys said petulantly into the phone. "I just think it would have been the courteous thing to do."

"Did Jenny ask for me?" Aviva queried, knowing good and well that Jenny was probably getting so much attention she hadn't had time to miss her mother.

"No, not exactly. But I know she was wondering why she hadn't heard from you," Gladys answered.

"Now, Gladys, how do you know that?" Aviva chuckled into the phone.

"I just know, Missy," she retorted, then quickly changed the subject. "Now tell me, how is everything in Los Angeles?"

Ah, here it is. It didn't take her long to get to the heart of the matter, Aviva thought. "All right, I guess." She couldn't resist arousing Gladys's curiosity just a little bit more. When silence greeted her admission she went on, truthfully this time, "Better than all right, Gladys. Jeremy's home is lovely and I am truly happy that I came."

"That's all? Truly happy you went?" Gladys demanded.

"That's it. I'm sorry to disappoint you but I haven't even been here twenty-four hours yet. I'll be able to give you the real scoop by tomorrow for sure," Aviva teased.

"Well, if that's all you have to tell me I might as well put your daughter on. Hold on and I'll get her," Gladys said, then added, "Oh, and Aviva..."

"Yes?"

"Give it the best you've got." Gladys just couldn't resist one more bit of advice.

"I will, Gladys," Aviva said with a sigh. "Now, could you please put Jenny on?"

She waited after Gladys said her good-byes and went to find Jenny. Lost in her daydreams, she didn't notice the door of the den open and Jeremy slip in. It was only when he surprised her by putting a steaming mug of coffee under her nose that she cocked her head and looked up into his dancing eyes. A kiss to her forehead accompanied the welcome gift, and Aviva closed her eyes to enjoy the gesture.

"Did you get Jenny on the phone?" Jeremy whispered, not wishing to disturb her if she was listening to her daughter.

"I got Gladys first and an earful about what a miserable creature I am for not calling her first thing to tell her all about our first day together," Aviva whispered back just in case someone was within hearing distance on the other end of the line.

Jeremy turned his eyes heavenward, a deep, short laugh escaping his lips as he did so. He looked wonderful. His jeans hugged every curve of him and was the only covering he wore. Aviva enjoyed watching him. He seemed so relaxed, at home, padding about shirtless and shoeless. It was most difficult, though, keeping her eyes off his chest. He had just the right amount of curling black hair sprinkled in the hollow where her lips had played only a few hours before.

"I hope you reported that we were getting along

famously," he said, disturbing her sensual thoughts.

"Of course not!" Aviva said, enjoying the look on his face, "I told her I might be home on the next plane if things didn't improve."

"Is that so?" he retorted, his face transforming itself into a look he considered to be a lecherous grin. Unfortunately, his efforts were more amusing than threatening, and Aviva tried to stifle her giggle as he came toward her.

Looking about, she tried to find someplace to put her coffee cup and finding none brought her knees up to her chest trying desperately to protect herself. But the effort was useless as Jeremy gently pounced on her, burying his face in the crook of her neck, his hands tickling her ribs through the cotton of his shirt that she still wore from the night before.

"Jeremy, don't," Aviva protested weakly through her giggles, "Jenny will be on the phone in a minute. Jeremy!" But her protests were useless as he continued to nibble on her neck, and she decided she didn't want to protest any longer. Aviva turned her head, holding the phone away from her as she did so, and moved her lips to meet the smooth plane of his brow, planting little kisses wherever she could.

"Mommy, hello." Suddenly Aviva sat up straight, her movement toppling Jeremy off the chair and onto the floor as she heard her daughter's voice.

"Hello, darling...yes, I'm here," she said, blushing though she knew there was no reason to. It was not as if Jenny had walked in on their love play.

Jeremy was standing before her rubbing his behind in an exaggerated manner; then slipping into the chair beside her, he put his ear up to the receiver and yelled into the phone.

"Jenny, hello; it's me, Jeremy."

"Jeremy, Jeremy." Jenny could hardly contain her excitement when she heard his greeting. "Jeremy, next time can I come for a visit, too?"

"Of course you can, little one," he said, obviously delighted by the response.

"When? When?" she asked insistently.

"I don't know. Whenever your mother says you can," he said. Watching Aviva shake her head "no" he simply smiled at her.

"How could you?" Aviva hissed at him good-naturedly. "She'll never let me rest now." In response Jeremy only shrugged his shoulders, and Aviva moved the phone closer to her mouth so that he wouldn't have an opportunity to promise Jenny anything else.

As mother and daughter spoke, Jeremy's hand played across Aviva's bare thigh, making it increasingly difficult for her to keep her mind on her conversation. What was she saying? Be good? Mind Sue? What did it matter? Aviva knew she had to get off the phone or Jenny might hear more than just motherly warnings about her behavior.

"All right, darling. I'll see you soon," Aviva said, finally ringing off.

Jeremy moved his hand for an instant, took her cup of coffee and set it on the floor as soon as she had hung up the phone. Putting his strong hands about her waist, he turned her toward him as if she were no more than a rag doll. Aviva placed her own small hands on his chest, twirling the dark hair between her fingers.

"That wasn't very nice, you know," she reprimanded him, her voice sultry.

"I know. Sometimes I'm not very nice. But this time it really wasn't my fault. I just couldn't resist. There's something about a woman in a man's shirt that just drives me crazy," he answered, kissing her lips.

"Oh? Just any woman?" she queried, turning her head so that his next kiss landed on her silky cheek.

"Of course. Young, old, short, tall..." he teased, never taking his lips far from her fair skin. "You didn't think you were anything special, did you?"

Aviva jumped from the chair in mock anger, attempting to run from his grasp, teach him a lesson for teasing her so. Though she was quick, she was not fast enough, and his hand shot out, catching the shirttail as she fled, pulling her back into his lap.

"Not just yet, my love," he said as the fingers of his free hand moved to the buttons of the shirt. "You must be taught not to be so gullible." In an instant his hand was inside the fabric, running merrily over her breasts as his lips once again assaulted hers.

This time there was no resistance and Aviva returned his kiss with an intensity that surprised her, her hands flying about his body with the same loving curiosity as his to hers. If this was a dream she never wanted to wake up. If Jeremy was anything other than a sensitive, adoring man she never wanted to find out.

The worn leather chair answered each of their pleasurable moans with a sigh of its own as they moved about trying desperately to find a comfortable spot in which they could enjoy their lovemaking. But comfort was not to be, and so, giggling and complaining and whispering words of love, they met there on the sticky covering and culminated their passionate game, collapsing in each other's arms to rest and touch with delicate curiosity.

"My coffee is cold," Aviva complained lightly when she finally lifted one of her hands from his warm chest.

"I'll make you some more."

"That's all right," she said, stretching aimlessly, then nestling back into the cradle of his arms. If only they could stay this way the entire week. Never go out, never do anything but hold each other, love each other. How safe she felt, how loved.

"What do you want to do today," Jeremy asked, opening his eyes, as if reading her thoughts. Aviva turned her green eyes up toward his, though she didn't know if he could read the pleading there, the silent pleading that he not force her to do anything, go anywhere. But Jeremy would not have it. He would not have her hiding herself there in the little bungalow.

"You know we have to do something. We'd wither away here if we didn't," he said, his voice gently stern.

"I don't mind, Jeremy. I can't think of anyone I would rather wither away with," Aviva answered, trying to dissuade him without asking outright.

"Aviva—" his hand reached up and smoothed the hair back from her face "—I know what you're thinking. I know that you want to hide here with me. But unless we go out there where the memories are we are not going to know if this will work. Do you understand?''

"Yes," she said as quietly as a child being forced to go to dance class.

"Do you agree with me?" he queried, unable to let the question rest.

"I guess. But we do have an entire week. Why do we have to go out today? Why can't we just wait a day or two?" she asked, hoping to change his mind.

"Because today is Saturday. Tomorrow is Sunday, and these are the only two days I have to spend with you all day. I do have to go to work, you know," he said, chucking her under the chin.

"You do?" For some reason Aviva hadn't really considered what would happen during the weekdays. She just assumed that Jeremy had cleared the entire week for her.

"Now, don't look like that. You're a big girl. I cleared as much time as I could but I just couldn't drop everything," Jeremy explained.

"But I did," Aviva retorted, hurt that he seemed to think less of her business than of his own.

"That's different—" Jeremy started to explain but Aviva didn't let him finish.

"What do you mean, that's different?" Quickly she jumped from the chair and glared down at Jeremy, her hands resting on her naked hips. "Do you think the inn is any less important than your business? How dare you..."

Just as quickly Jeremy was up on his feet, his hands

grabbing her shoulders. Though she tried to jerk away he would not let her, and quickly his arms encircled her angry form, rendering her helpless.

"Aviva, calm down. I didn't say that, did I?" He waited for an answer and Aviva was forced to shake her head reluctantly. "All right. What I meant was that on such short notice there was only so much time I could take off. I'm delighted that you were able to get away for a whole week. I just couldn't rearrange everything that quickly. It has nothing to do with whose work is more important. Do you understand?" She raised her eyes to meet his. Looking into the black depths she realized he was right. How could she be so silly? It was almost as if she were looking for an excuse to pick a fight.

"Oh, Jeremy." She sighed, ashamed of her outburst. "I'm so sorry. I don't know why I said those things."

"I do," he answered, stroking her hair. "I know you're nervous. But look, you've made the first step. Let's take the other steps together. So far I haven't turned into the monster you thought I would, have I?" Again she shook her head. "Well, then, let's take the next step and see if I melt when I get in the sunlight. All right?"

"Okay," she said, finally smiling up at him, though her heart still didn't want to accept what he was suggesting. If only he would give her a little more time.

"Great." His hold on her loosened but Aviva did not move away from him, preferring his warmth and security to her own autonomy at the moment. "Now, go take a shower and decide where you want to go. If you don't have any ideas I'll make up your mind for you," he warned, turning her around and sending her to the bathroom with a pat on the rear.

Aviva stood for a long time allowing the warm water to course over her as she considered where they should spend the day. Her first instinct was to choose anywhere but the haunts where she and Sam had spent their time. She knew that visiting downtown Beverly Hills or lunching on Santa Monica Boulevard or even seeing a movie in Hollywood would only increase the risk she was already taking by simply being in Southern California.

Perhaps she should suggest a ride down to Long Beach to see the *Queen Mary* or maybe to Venice Beach to watch the crazy roller skaters. She considered her options, then stepped out of the shower.

Springtime in Southern California was quite different from the same season in its northern sister, and the weather was warm enough for a simple khaki outfit. One last look in the mirror and she went in search of Jeremy, her decision still not made but her spirits a great deal better.

She found him in the little garden off the bedroom. He, too, had changed, and Aviva smiled when she saw that he had chosen an outfit similar to hers. They looked like twins except for the color of their shirts. Hers was green, to match her eyes, his a rich navy blue. Turning at the sound of her giggle, Jeremy immediately caught on to the joke.

"It looks like we planned this, doesn't it?" he said, smiling ruefully.

"As a matter of fact, it does. But we're not out to

impress anyone, are we?" Aviva asked, the hopeful note in her voice far too evident.

"Of course not," Jeremy countered. "At least I can assure you that I am not." She breathed a sigh of relief knowing that she would have to stop testing him. After all, she was sure that even Jeremy Crowley had a breaking point and his patience with her would not last forever.

"What have you got there?" Aviva asked as she approached him, trying to steer their conversation away from her silly concerns.

"Just some dead flowers," Jeremy answered, turning slightly to indicate the pansies growing in neat little rows. "You know the plant will remain much healthier if you do this periodically."

"I wouldn't know. When we lived here we didn't have a garden and, well, at the inn we just let everything grow naturally." Aviva felt a sudden twinge of homesickness when she mentioned the inn, and Jeremy came to put his arms around her.

"You miss it, don't you?" he asked, nuzzling her neck.

"I do. Isn't that silly, though? I haven't been gone that long but there is something—the activity, I guess—that I miss." Thinking better of her wanderings, she added, "But I love being here, too. Your home is so quiet, so peaceful. It really is lovely, Jeremy."

"Yes, it is. I take great pride in it. But I'm not going to let you talk me into staying in our happy nest, much as I would like to." His hands moved to her waist and he gave her a quick little squeeze before turning her around, draping his arm over her shoulders and leading her toward the kitchen. Keys in hand, he asked her once again. "Now, where to, my lady?"

"Jeremy, I really don't know. Why don't you choose? After all, the whole idea of this trip is so that we get to know each other. I've told you all about me. If you choose where we are to spend the day, then I'll know something more about you." Why hadn't she thought of it before? It was a perfect solution. After all, she wasn't exactly here visiting a relative who would take her to Disneyland. She did want to know about him and depending on where he chose to take her she would begin to find the answers to her questions regarding the true personality of Jeremy Crowley.

"All right, then. But I warn you, I intend to be masterful and I will not change my mind no matter how you beg and plead." Quickly he whisked her out the door and settled her into the Mercedes.

As they drove, Aviva's mind drifted back to the last time she sat in this car. It was here in this seat that she had heard Jeremy promise her that what they had was worth pursuing. It was in this seat that her heart had told her the whole idea was impossible.

Yet look at her now. She was there, with him in Los Angeles, and he was as attentive and charming and loving as he had been at the inn. Maybe nothing was impossible. Maybe what she had thought was too good to be true actually was happening. Perhaps Jeremy Crowley was one of those unusual people one sometimes met in a great metropolis like Los Angeles: a powerful, successful man who was untouched by the plastic mentality of those around him.

She felt at ease riding in the familiar car, listening to his familiar litany of amusing events. If she closed her eyes she could almost believe that they were on their way back to the inn, where they would sit with a glass of brandy and talk until the wee hours of the morning.

"Here we are," Jeremy announced, disturbing her train of thought. Aviva looked about her. Camden Drive—the heart of Beverly Hills. What were they doing there?

"Where are we?" Aviva asked, her nervousness rising.

"At my office. I thought you might like to get a firsthand view of what it is I actually do for a living." Opening the door he stepped out and came around the car to get her.

There were people everywhere, darting in and out of the expensive shops. Well-dressed, well-heeled men and women, all with the look of money about them. Not much had changed in Beverly Hills. Still the beautiful people flocked to pay outrageous prices for the clothing, china and jewelry that could be found in the small, elite city.

Before she could say a word about the hustle and bustle of the city, Jeremy whisked her into the small building directly in front of the car. The elevator was so tiny it could only hold three or four people comfortably.

"I think you work in a building made for Munchkins," Aviva observed.

"Everything in Beverly Hills is getting smaller. No

one can afford too much space," Jeremy answered
without rancor. "But it's still one of the best business
addresses to have. People seem to think that your
work is better if your address is here."

"I know what you mean. Some people are so stupid."

"Now, I don't want to hear any of that kind of talk.
Perhaps others aren't quite as practical as you are but
you have to allow them their little eccentricities." Jeremy's reprimands were getting tiresome. Why did he
always have to give everyone the benefit of the
doubt? Was she really such a horrible person for
calling things as she saw them? Thinking again,
though, Aviva realized that she was really letting this
L.A. thing become an obsession and she promised
herself to try to be a bit more understanding.

Just then, the elevator door opened and they were
standing in one of the most charming lobbies Aviva
had ever seen. Taking her elbow Jeremy led her
through the office room by room explaining that the
suite had actually been a young ladies' charm school
before he took it over. Aviva was thrilled that he had
left many of the original accoutrements, including the
lovely wallpaper in the bathroom and the outdoor furniture on the little balcony overlooking Camden
Drive. The office was as tastefully intimate as Jeremy's house, and Aviva immediately felt at home
there. She leaned over a large drawing table with sincere interest as Jeremy showed her blueprints for a
hospital he was working on in Sacramento. There was
even a project in Alaska. It seemed as if he worked
everywhere and anywhere.

"You're not here very often, from the looks of it," Aviva commented when they finally put the drawings away.

"No, I'm not, and I think my staff is grateful for that. I'm a real slave driver," he answered, making light of an obviously successful business.

"That's not what Kelly tells me. She thinks the world of you." Aviva was proud that the kindness he had shown her obviously carried over to others as well. With every passing minute her concerns about Jeremy faded more and more until they were only mere shadows in her mind. Finally she was able to relax and enjoy his company to the fullest.

"I can see now why you have to work next week. Your time must be in great demand when you're here."

"I'm afraid it is. Aviva, I really am sorry that I wasn't able to clear the whole week. I hope you know that." He turned serious eyes on her.

"Of course I do. Now just be patient with me."

"I can't think of anything more I'd like to do. I told you once that I could wait, and I meant it." His hand reached out and touched her cheek, sealing his promise.

"And, sir, I will be eternally grateful for that." Aviva dipped a curtsy, not wishing the conversation to get too heavy, with the whole day before them. The way she felt about him, they could have made love right there among the business plans and blueprints, but she knew that if their experiment were to work they would have to spend their time in other ways.

"Where to now?" Aviva asked before he could reach out and hold her as she knew he wanted to.

"Well, I'll bet it's been a long time since you've been shopping on the streets of Beverly Hills. What do you say we take in the local sights?" he asked brightly.

"Sounds good to me," Aviva agreed with a little more bravado than she felt.

As they walked up and down Rodeo Drive, Beverly Drive and Camden Drive, Aviva found that she truly was enjoying herself. In Giorgio's she tried on a simple taffeta dirndl and twirled before Jeremy, who sipped his complimentary cocktail as he nodded his approval. It was only when Aviva's face went ashen as she looked at the price tag that he approached her, asking if anything was wrong. Seeing the price, even Jeremy gasped in disbelief and good-naturedly ordered her out of the skirt before anything happened to it.

When Jeremy waltzed her into Bijan past the guard, Aviva was overly impressed. Obviously Jeremy must be someone of consequence since Bijan showed its wares by appointment only. It was the most exclusive shop in Beverly Hills, complete with gold derringers and mink-lined raincoats. Then at the UNICEF store Aviva found a beautiful handmade stuffed bear and decided to purchase it for Jenny. After all, the cost of the toy went to a good cause. It was the only item in any of the stores that Aviva could buy in good conscience.

Finally, at one o'clock, both Jeremy and Aviva expressed their hunger almost simultaneously. Taking her hand Jeremy led her to R.J.'s for Ribs, the best rib joint in Los Angeles. Aviva thought she could never have a better time no matter what happened the rest of her life. Jeremy's constant touches, the soft whispers of love when she least expected them, served only to make the day more glorious than she ever thought it could be.

"Jeremy, this has been a fantastic day," she said, finally leaning back in the booth when she finished the last tasty morsel. "I can't remember when I've had a better time. Do you think Jenny will like the stuffed toy I got her?"

"No doubt about it," Jeremy answered without hesitation. Then leaning across the table, he took her hand in his. "And I am so happy that you finally relaxed. I was beginning to think I'd never see the Aviva I treasure outside the walls of my house."

"Was I that bad?" She frowned, knowing that she had given him more than cause for concern.

"Not really. It's just that—" Aviva never heard the last of his sentence because the next words to reach her ears did not come from Jeremy's lips.

"Jeremy!" The voice, gratingly low and measured, was like a blow to the stomach for Aviva. Looking up, panic in her eyes, she saw Diane Chesterfield standing before them.

"Diane," Jeremy answered, his voice open and friendly, "so nice to see you again."

"It has been ages, darling. You weren't at Katie's last week, and we didn't see you at the club for the tournament. We all thought you had fallen off the face of the earth. But now I can see you've definitely fallen, but a little closer to home." Diane's ice-blue eyes turned and lit on Aviva, appraising the younger woman openly. "You've brought little Aviva back to the fold, I see."

Aviva's mouth opened slightly but no words came out. She was in limbo, caught between the present and the past. For a moment she thought that if she looked over to her luncheon companion, she would see Sam sitting there, Sam with his eyes raking over Diane's figure and face. With the greatest determination Aviva forced herself to look. Her heart slowed. It was Jeremy, and his eyes weren't stripping the clothes off the woman who had so suddenly appeared, but he was speaking to her, smiling at her.

"Aviva is here on a visit." She was grateful he had filled the void, knowing she should have answered Diane but somehow unable to.

"That's wonderful. How is your inn these days, Aviva?" Again the woman turned toward her and waited for an answer.

"Fine" was all that Aviva could muster. It was as if Diane had mesmerized her. All she could do was look—look at the frizz of carefully coiffed platinum curls that surrounded Diane's well-tended face. The salons certainly had done their job well. Diane didn't look a day over thirty-five, though Aviva knew full well the woman was closer to forty-five.

Aviva felt like a schoolgirl sitting under the spell of something foreign, sophisticated and somehow evil. Diane's white cashmere sweater covered her from shoulder to hip like a giant white bubble, and Aviva found herself wondering if the woman ever wore pants that didn't look as if they had been painted on. The outfit must have cost her a fortune, but something was not right, something was askew. Then suddenly Aviva's ears perked up. What was Jeremy saying? She must break in and stop him.

"Of course we'd be delighted to come." He was speaking to Diane, accepting some sort of invitation for both of them.

"That's wonderful, darling. Now don't disappoint us Monday night. There are so many who are just dying to see you again," Diane purred, reaching out one of her talonlike nails to brush Jeremy's chin. Aviva's anger rose when she realized that he had not pulled away from her as he should have. How dare he accept Diane's advances? How dare he accept her invitation knowing how she disliked the woman?

"We'll be looking forward to seeing you, too, Aviva dear. I'm sure there will be so many people you know. George is waiting. I've got to run, darlings. See you Monday night."

For the first time Aviva noticed the man who waited impatiently by the door and began to speak the moment Diane joined him. His face was familiar to Aviva but she couldn't place him, didn't want to place him as she turned her angry attention back to Jeremy.

"How about some of their three-foot cake?" he asked innocently, returning to their conversation as if Diane had never been there. But she had, and Aviva was not going to let things go that easily.

"How could you?" she hissed through clenched teeth. If they hadn't been in a restaurant Aviva was sure that she would have tried to claw his eyes out. Not just for accepting Diane's invitation but for the kind way he treated her, just as if she were Gladys or a shopkeeper in Carmel. She would have clawed his eyes out just for not knowing how angry and hurt she was.

"How could I what?" His expression was serious and registered genuine surprise.

"Accept her invitation, that's what. You know how I feel about her and her crowd. You know that she caused me the biggest hurt of my life. How could you..." Aviva could not finish her sentence and in pure exasperation threw down her napkin and headed for the door. But before she could get her bearings when she reached the street, Jeremy was upon her. Suddenly her shoulders were surrounded by his strong arm and he swiftly led her to an open doorway of an office building, allowing them some semblance of privacy.

Aviva shook her shoulders trying to disengage herself from him, but the more she struggled the stronger his hold became until her head came to rest on his chest as she gasped for breath between her tears. Emotionally drained from her sudden outburst, she was suddenly too tired to fight him anymore.

"Aviva," Jeremy began, gently trying to get her to raise her head, to look at him. "Aviva, look at me."

"No," she answered petulantly. "Just let me go. I just want to be alone for a little while."

"I'm not going to do that. That's how this whole thing started. When you left here, there was no one to tell you to stay and face your problems. No one to force you not to be alone. But I'm here now and I'm going to make you do just that, no matter how you hate me for it."

His lips met the top of her head and rained kisses on her silky hair as his hands stroked her back. Aviva was aware of the people passing. She heard laughter and bits of conversation, but all she could think about was that she wanted to be away from there, away—but in Jeremy's arms nonetheless.

"I won't hate you for it. But I don't understand why it's so important to you," she said through her sniffles.

"It's important because I want you to be the best you can be. I want you to be as strong as I know you are. Why flee from ghosts? They can't hurt you, not as long as I am with you." His words were soothing and Aviva felt herself succumbing to his logic. He was right. They couldn't hurt her anymore unless, unless...

"Jeremy," she said, her voice low. "I just don't want the ghosts to get you. I don't want you to become part of them, I don't want them to get to be part of you. Do you understand?"

"Yes, but trust me enough to let me prove to you that we can all live together. You just have to accept them for what they are. Not become a part of them. You know I enjoy Diane." Jeremy felt Aviva stiffen and he tightened his grasp on her. "I enjoy her company as I do the company of many of the other people we'll see at her house on Monday night. But it doesn't mean that my whole world revolves around them. Aviva, for me, say you will try to understand this. Say you'll give them and us a chance at that party." His voice was pleading and Aviva knew that everything he had said to her was right. But logic didn't matter in such situations. Feelings, emotions, those were the things that mattered because those were the things she lived with. Nothing he could say or do could change that.

Looking up now into the dark depths of his eyes, she realized that she would not fight him. Her love was too deep for her to disappoint him without at least trying to do what he asked. In her soul, though, she knew already that the experiment was hopeless. As much as she loved him she would not compromise everything. They would go to the party and she would give it her best shot, but if it didn't work... If it didn't work, then she would have to choose between Jeremy and Whaler's Inn, where her new life lay. Studying his face she wondered if he were strong enough to resist the temptations that lay ahead of them.

"All right, Jeremy, I'll try," she acquiesced, "but you don't know what they can do—"

He stopped her short. "I do know. You forget that I have known them as long as you have, if not longer. I can handle it."

"I hope you can, Jeremy" was all she said before letting her head once again rest on his shoulder. They stayed that way, holding each other until a man quietly excused himself, forcing them to vacate the doorway in embarrassment.

Jeremy put on a bright face and steered Aviva to the car, chattering the whole way, trying to get her mind off the unfortunate encounter. Aviva gladly went with him and let his words and jokes and caresses slowly push Diane's specter to the back of her mind. If nothing else, she was determined to end the day the way it began, by loving Jeremy Crowley, by pretending the whole incident had never happened.

The sun was beginning to set over Venice Beach when Jeremy parked the car in the empty lot and ran to open her door. The twenty-minute drive to the ocean had calmed her, and now she walked on the smooth wet sand, hand in hand with the man she loved, in peace.

They had rolled their khakis to their knees and played tag with the gentle swells that rolled onto the beach. Every once in a while a dog and its master or mistress would come jogging down the dark sand, parting Aviva and Jeremy for only a moment. Then, hand in hand, the lovers continued their leisurely trek.

"Aviva," Jeremy said when they stood quietly watching the sun become an orange ball of flame over the horizon.

"Hm?" She lifted her head from his shoulder and moved her lips so that they brushed his hand.

"Will you marry me?" he asked simply, the straightforward question surprising her.

Looking up, she studied his profile. Had he asked her that morning, had they never taken the fateful trip into Beverly Hills or met Diane along the way she would have been overjoyed. But now concerns nipped at her heart, the hurt forgotten so long had opened up again and left her unsure of what she should say, how far she should commit herself.

"Where would we live? I would have to do something with the inn and I don't know if I would want to really leave it. Then there's the matter of school for

Jenny and—'' Her words were tripping over one another, she spoke so fast. Aviva had no desire to bring up the meeting with Diane and was hoping that by raising all the other questions she could keep herself from expressing her real concern. But the trick didn't work and the unwanted words poured from her lips. "And I don't know if I want to live here. See people like Diane and—''

Suddenly her objections were squelched as his lips met hers in an urgent kiss. Turning toward him, Aviva captured his neck with her arms and clung to him as if to a life raft in the middle of a turbulent ocean.

"Aviva,'' he said when they finally parted, "if there were no inn, no Jenny, no Diane, if there were nothing but the two of us, would you marry me here and now? Please, humor me just this once. Would you?'' His eyes searched her face. It seemed as if he needed to know, needed to be told he was loved. Jeremy Crowley, she thought, was sure that he could take care of anything else, solve any other problem, and it was that confidence Aviva saw in his dancing eyes. It was the confidence she wished she could share.

As the sun dipped below the horizon she surrendered and allowed her mind to play his game. Determined to believe that the question was so simple, determined to allow herself the pleasure of having him without the intrusion of Diane or the party or the thought of losing the inn, Aviva answered him.

"Yes, my love, I would marry you tonight. I would love you forever,'' she said, allowing her lips once again to find his, curtailing any further discussion he might have wanted to have on the subject. It would be enough that he knew the purity of her love. If in all the world there was just him, she would never want for anything. But there was more to the world than that, and she would have to face it. But not then, not that night. Aviva knew she would not even consider anything or anyone else until she was forced to. It was a long time before they parted and, holding hands tightly as if they might lose each other on the deserted sandy beach, they made their way back to the car and headed for the haven of Jeremy's small house.

Chapter Nine

Jeremy was a magician. Sunday came and went and Aviva never once thought of the party Diane was throwing Monday night. He kept her so busy sightseeing, loving, cooking, talking that she didn't have one moment to consider how she was going to handle the impending showdown with her old world. Jeremy had wrapped her in a blanket so safe, so secure, that she was sure nothing could touch her. It was as if they had never left the hearth of Whaler's Inn, except their hideaway there in Jeremy's little house was much quieter without Jenny's constant interruptions and Gladys's curiosity.

Not until Aviva, restless in the night despite the draining lovemaking that they had pursued, turned to look at the lighted dial of the clock and noticed that it was already 3:00 A.M. did she even think of Diane.

Who else, she wondered, would be there at the cocktail party? The men Sam had known who had thought nothing of making advances to her, the women whose advances were welcomed by her husband? What did it matter who attended? Even if Diane were the only one Aviva saw, it would be enough because she was the last woman Sam had been with. She epitomized everything Aviva hated about Los Angeles and the fast-paced world she had left behind.

Quietly turning once more, she reached out and stroked Jeremy's sleeping face. Gently so as not to wake him she let her fingers trace the contours of his cheeks, revel in the silkiness of his tousled hair. He looked like an angel in the shadows playing over his sleeping form. Her heart swelled in her breast and she felt the tears well up in her eyes. Tears of love, tears of frustration. She dared not voice her concerns once more for fear of driving him away from her, even though she knew deep in her mind that he would listen and console her. She just wanted to be stronger for him. Aviva knew she would do her best. She just hoped it was enough. But Jeremy would have to understand if it wasn't. He would have to accept whatever came.

Finally, rolling onto her back, Aviva slung one long and slender arm over her eyes and prayed for sleep to take her. Take her it did. Gently, swiftly, without her knowledge, so that she slept despite Jeremy's slipping from the warm confines of the bed, kissing her lightly once he was dressed, and shutting the bedroom door carefully behind him as he left for the office.

It was ten o'clock when Aviva woke to the ringing of the telephone. With a groan she grabbed a pillow and buried her head underneath it. But the ringing persisted, and she reached for the receiver, never thinking that she wasn't in her own home and that perhaps she shouldn't be answering the phone at all.

"Don't tell me you're still asleep?" Jeremy chuckled into the phone. Immediately awake, Aviva sat up in the bed with a start, aware that she should be grateful it was Jeremy on the other end of the line.

"Jeremy, I'm sorry. Maybe I shouldn't have answered..." she began, embarrassed that she had not thought before taking action.

"Don't be silly. If I didn't want you to answer the phone, I wouldn't have called, would I?" That made sense, and Aviva relaxed, snuggling deeply into the rumpled covers.

"Of course, you're right. What time did you leave?"

"About eight. I kissed you good-bye and didn't even get so much as a smile. Is this how it's going to be if we tie the knot?" he asked, his voice carrying a more serious message than the teasing tone would indicate.

"Never. If we were married I'd probably never let you go to work," Aviva answered. The idea of living with Jeremy had become more palatable with each passing minute they were together. He had been right when he told her, so long ago now, that no matter where they were he was still the same person.

"I hope that's a promise," he countered, "but enough of such frivolous prattle—"

"Jeremy, I would hardly call discussing our almost-future frivolous prattle!" Aviva objected strenuously.

"Just kidding, darling," he apologized briefly before continuing. "I just wanted to let you know that I'm going to be later than I thought tonight. I hope you don't mind that we won't have time for dinner before the party.''

Suddenly all the thoughts of her early-morning meanderings came flooding back. Oh, why couldn't he have waited until the last minute to remind her about Diane's party, she thought with a sinking heart.

"Aviva, all I hear is silence. How about answering the question, or are you having heart failure?''

"I'm sorry, I guess I'm still asleep," she lied, not wanting him to know the truth. She had promised herself she would give the evening her best shot and she meant it. "Of course, that's fine. I don't mind eating later. Diane'll probably have a feast anyway.'' Her vain attempt at humor fell flat and she found herself blushing even though she was alone.

"You're right," Jeremy agreed. "Listen, I've got to run, so I'll pick you up at seven sharp.'' Aviva agreed to be ready and was afraid that Jeremy would ring off without so much as an "I love you," but she should have known better.

"Aviva," he called out as if he thought she would hang up.

"Yes?''

"I love you and—'' he hesitated "—I'm proud that you'll be with me tonight.''

"Thank you, Jeremy," Aviva said, grateful to him for the kind words of encouragement. "I love you, too. See you tonight.''

From that instant on, Aviva moved like lightning to keep her mind off the party. Her shower must have set a world record and she cleaned the house till it sparkled. It felt wonderful straightening Jeremy's house. Had he been one of those men who expected it, Aviva would have simply let things be. But because he had treated her like a queen, it was the least she could do.

By the time noon rolled around she had exhausted all her outlets around the house. Unfortunately, reading did not seem to keep her mind from wandering, and she finally decided to take advantage of Jeremy's offer to use his second car. Grabbing the keys he had left her and her purse, she made her way to the garage and lifted the heavy door.

Her mouth fell open in surprise as she saw the fire-engine red Jaguar hidden behind the door. He certainly had a penchant for fancy cars, she mused as she walked around it, looking for any sign of a dent or scratch. There wasn't one and she thought twice about taking it. If she managed to even get a speck of dust on its gleaming exterior, Aviva was sure that she would die of embarrassment.

Gathering her courage, she slid into the deep bucket seat and sat for a moment caressing the leather-covered steering wheel. She had never felt quite the same way when she sat in the Mercedes she and Sam had owned, perhaps because she often felt he cared more for the beautiful car than for her.

Finally, throwing caution to the winds, she turned the key in the ignition and backed the car out into the quiet street. Soon Aviva and the car were one. She felt free and sexy and wonderfully cared for, and she let her thoughts dwell on Jeremy and the wonderful life that was ahead of them.

He had been right: they could work anything out. She felt invincible, a feeling she was going to hang on to no matter who was at Diane's party. She was going to beat them all.

As she sat at a stoplight, lost in her daydreams filled with images of Jeremy, Aviva didn't notice for a moment where she was. The driving had been so therapeutic that she had turned and turned and never really paid attention to where she was going. But suddenly something caught her eye and immediately her plans for the future disappeared. It was disturbing, frightening, an unwanted memory, but for a moment she couldn't focus on the source of her discontent.

The place looked so familiar. Long stone walls stretched for half a mile in either direction. A wrought-iron fence stood open, beckoning to her. Then she saw it: a small brass sign. It was the back entrance to the cemetery where Sam was buried, Aviva realized with sudden horror.

Almost against her will her hands gripped the steering wheel and turned the car into the drive that wound through the impeccably kept grounds. Slowly she steered the automobile as her eyes darted from hill to hill. There it was. She couldn't see the simple headstone from where she parked the car, but Aviva knew that it was the right place.

Out of the car, her feet carried her over the soft grass until she stood staring down at the grave. A collage of remembrances burst upon her mind, stumbling over one another. Aviva waited—waited for tears or anger or sorrow to invade her heart and soul. But nothing came. Nothing but understanding, finally, of who Sam was, why she had loved him, why she had hated him.

Understanding was a wonderful thing. Growing from an experience didn't hurt at all. But standing there, alone with him once more, Aviva knew that she would never again allow herself to be in the same situation. She could look at the world clearly now. Whaler's Inn had given her the strength to do that— the responsibility, the success, which had been hers alone.

"It's all right now, Sam," she whispered. "I can go on from here. You'd like Jeremy. In some ways he's a lot like you. If he turns out to be like you in other ways, I think I can handle it. I can stand on my own two feet now, you know." She stood there for only a minute longer, then turned and left without ever looking back.

SHE HAD CHOSEN her outfit so carefully, but now that she heard Jeremy's key in the door she felt a pang of uncertainty.

Enough of that now, she scolded herself and went to greet him.

"Darling, you look wonderful." The first words out of his mouth thrilled her and she went running to him and planted a kiss directly on his waiting lips. Jeremy grabbed her hands and held her away from him, appraising her appreciatively. Then he released her and she twirled about, the lavender knit dress clinging to her shapely legs as she stood on her toes in her delicate mole-colored sandals.

"How jealous they will all be tonight," Jeremy continued, reaching for her once more and effectively kissing away her lipstick.

"I don't want anyone to be jealous, Jeremy," Aviva said, suddenly serious. "I just want us to enjoy ourselves and come back exactly the way we left—in love with each other."

"I couldn't agree more. Shall we go?"

Though she had known Diane for years, Aviva had no idea where she lived. She knew, though, that wherever it was, it was certain to be spectacular. Therefore, when Jeremy stopped in front of a beautiful Georgian manor reminiscent of a hotel, Aviva wasn't surprised. Taking a deep breath as Jeremy helped her from the car, she squared her shoulders and allowed him to lead her up the walk.

"Jeremy, darling." Diane didn't give them a second to catch their breath once they walked through the door. She was on them like a spider after its prey. "We thought you'd never arrive."

"Diane, it's only seven-thirty. The party started at seven." Jeremy laughed at her wiles, pulling Aviva a little closer to give her courage.

"Ah, I see you've brought Aviva with you. Have you been enjoying your stay?" she asked, her lips curling into what passed for a smile.

Before Aviva could answer, Diane had linked her arm through Jeremy's and was leading him into the well-peopled living room, with Jeremy dragging Aviva along with them.

Her heart sank when she recognized more than half the people in the room—starlets, commercial directors, advertising people. As Diane whisked them about the room, Jeremy greeted most of them warmly and Aviva squeezed his arm even more for protection. Most of them recognized her, too, and a few offered their condolences over Sam's death. Aviva bristled at such false concern. Where had they been when he died, she wondered, feeling her anger welling. But then, looking at Jeremy, who continued giving her looks of encouragement, she pushed her feelings down to the pit of her stomach and was as pleasant as she could be.

An hour passed with no problems. Aviva was almost enjoying herself. The food and wine were excellent, and Jeremy had been an angel standing guard by her side until she had acclimated herself. But he had been gone almost half an hour now, and she still stood holding an empty wineglass, alone in a corner.

Carefully she watched the people around her. Nothing had changed. In a barely lit corner she noticed a group of Diane's guests sharing a vial of cocaine. Women and men were pairing off, the conversation becoming louder.

"Aviva." She looked toward the voice and saw Stan Channing coming her way. He was the biggest womanizer in Los Angeles, a "good friend" of Sam's, even though he hadn't bothered to even send a condolence note to her when Sam died.

"Stan." Aviva greeted him, gritting her teeth as she smiled halfheartedly.

"Well, it's nice to see a new face at one of Diane's parties. You're looking lovely."

"I'm hardly what you'd call a new face," Aviva said, trying to keep the conversation civil.

"Well, even when you were married to Sam we hardly ever saw you." His hand reached up and captured her shoulder, pulling her closer to him. "I'm awfully glad you're back. I always wanted to get to know you better. You know what we used to call you?" Aviva shook her head, inching away from him, not really caring what any of them used to call her.

"The Snow Queen," he answered despite her silence, pulling her back in to him, "but that was before we got into the coke. Sorry, but you had to give up the title then." His hand was snaking down her shoulder playing with her collarbone.

"Stan, I don't really care," she said, taking his hand and removing it from her shoulder.

"Same old Aviva. Never did know how to have any fun," he said, sneering at her. "You ought to take a lesson from your new friend. Jeremy there knows how to be nice to people. He always seems to have a good time. You better get used to it if you're going to be hanging around him." With that Stan left.

Aviva felt her skin crawl underneath her dress where Stan had touched her. How dare he talk to her in that manner? Though she had always suspected that she had been the center of unkind conversation, she never imagined that anyone would have the audacity to spell it out so clearly. Where was Jeremy? She had to get away from here!

Finally she saw him. A young blond woman was hanging on his arm as he tried to balance two glasses of wine. He looked uncomfortable yet spoke to her, his charming smile flashing now and again. Moving from her corner, angry at Stan Channing for reminding her exactly why she had hated Sam's friends and their life in Los Angeles, Aviva went to rescue Jeremy.

"Jeremy, can I help you with those?" she said, startling the young woman on his arm.

"Thanks, honey. Here's yours." He handed her one glass and turned to his companion, "Aviva, I want you to meet Kitty. Kitty, Aviva." Aviva nodded her hello, then turned to Jeremy.

"Jeremy, I think it's time we were going," Aviva said, trying to keep the tension out of her voice.

"It's only eight-thirty, honey. We're just getting started here," Jeremy said, smiling his glorious smile and planting a kiss on her cheek before turning back to the woman he called Kitty.

Aviva's mouth fell open. Could it be he didn't want to leave, didn't see how the evening was progressing? Perhaps what Aviva had construed as discomfort was only the inability to handle two glasses and Kitty. Surely he could see what was going on, she thought angrily. In another hour the place would be a shambles. Everyone's wife or date would have felt ten hands on her shoulder or patting her rear end. Every husband would have been flattered by a pass that was usually only an entrée to bigger and better games.

"Jeremy, I really would like to go home," she persisted, hoping that he would understand and lead her out of the house away from all the beautiful people.

"Aviva, I would like to stay," he said evenly, his eyes indicating that he had no intention of leaving the party. Then turning toward the blonde, he excused them both and led Aviva to a semiquiet corner.

"Aviva, what is wrong? I thought you agreed to give this a fighting chance," he said.

Looking into his eyes she saw that he was not angry by her insistence but he was also not pleased. "Stan Channing just made a pass at me, and when I shrugged him off he was very rude," she defended herself, her eyes pleading with Jeremy to take her home.

"Stan makes passes at everyone. You have to learn to roll with the punches. Find someone you enjoy talking to. Aviva, you've got to try." He attempted to reason with her, oblivious to her discomfort. "You really haven't given this a chance yet. I still want to talk to a few people about a couple of projects, and then we'll go, okay?"

"Okay," she answered sullenly.

"Come with me if you want." Jeremy offered her his arm but she declined. "Honey, I do want you to have a good time. I'm not keeping you here out of spite, you know."

"I know. I just don't want to stay."

"I'm sorry. I have to insist. If we're going to be married you're going to have to get used to going to these parties at least once in a while. I won't force you. It's not as if we're going to make the rounds, but I will have to attend things like this and I want you with me. I love you, Aviva—never forget that." Kissing her lightly, he left her, offering her a reassuring hug before he went.

Aviva stood alone for a few moments. She didn't want to be a burden to him, didn't want to stand by his elbow like a frightened child, didn't want him to have to protect her. She could take care of herself; she simply didn't want to make the effort with these people. Was that so wrong?

Finding her way to the stairwell, she settled herself on the bottom step and sipped her wine. Jeremy was not being unreasonable, she knew. If they did get married, going to parties like this every now and then would not be punishment. He did understand how she felt. He just couldn't believe that she was so adamant in her refusal to even try to fit in.

Yet, just as much as he was trying to change her wasn't she trying to change him by attempting to take him away from a situation he obviously enjoyed? Oh, none of it was fair. None of it made sense. Looking at him through the doorway, Aviva saw him laughing and talking with a group of people. He was naturally gregarious. It was part of what she loved about him. And he was different from the other people in the room. His face shone with a healthy glow. He drank lightly, didn't use drugs. Everything about him was so perfect except for this: this light "fix" he needed every now and then—not drugs but people. She couldn't blame him. She couldn't stop loving him. But she also knew she couldn't possibly live with him in this environment.

Aviva knew positively now that her home was at the inn. She never again wanted her lunch to be interrupted by Diane Chesterfield. She never again wanted to have to attend parties like this—even once a year. Or, heaven forbid, to be a hostess at one. Aviva would not give up everything she worked for to be even a small part of this again. She knew the moment she sold the inn and moved Jenny back here that her resentment toward Jeremy would grow with each necessary encounter with this group. And this was necessary—for his business and for his happiness. She would not change him but she would not let him change her, either.

Suddenly the atmosphere was too intense. Her skin began to tingle and she felt frantic, anxious to leave the place. With new resolve Aviva rose and went to Jeremy's side. Like a caged animal nervous to get out for a run, she stood by his side until she could whisper in his ear.

"Jeremy, I must go now," she said, her voice strained. Turning, he looked deeply into her eyes and held her gaze for what seemed like an eternity. Without saying good-bye to their hostess, he took Aviva's arm and led her out to the car quietly, with no outward sign of anger, just silent resignation.

THEY LAY side by side, not touching. It was the first time since they had known each other that they had not even been able to talk. Aviva felt Jeremy's frustration and confusion and wondered if he understood her behavior that evening, if he could forgive what he must consider her rude and childish actions.

But how could he not understand? He knew about Sam and Diane, he knew how she hated that whole crowd. Couldn't he believe that she had really tried at least to tolerate the entire scene around her? For an hour she had been pleasant. But it was like asking a sports fan to sit through an evening of ballet.

He had enjoyed himself, treating Diane and everyone else as if they mattered. Maybe to him they did. Didn't he tell her to accept them for what they were? But wasn't that a waste of energy? Wasn't that the same as saying he and she were just like the people at the party?

"Aviva?" His voice was questioning as he touched her arm, stirring her from her reverie. She steeled herself, feeling the familiar thrill run through her, not wanting to respond. "Talk to me."

She continued to stare at the ceiling. How could she ask him to give up the people he considered friends? She had asked Sam, and where had it gotten her? Only to be more alone than she had ever been in her life. She was not going to make the same mistake with Jeremy. She would have to choose and, with great sadness, she knew that her choice would be home and hearth without Jeremy Crowley. Unless...unless...

"Jeremy? Where will we live after we're married?" she asked, hoping against hope that he would give her an answer that would resolve the problem at hand.

He rolled over onto his side, his arm over her midriff, rubbing the slick silk of her gown back and forth over her skin. "I honestly don't know. Don't you think that's something we really have to discuss, work out together?"

Aviva nodded her head so slightly in the darkened room that it would have been a wonder if Jeremy knew what her answer had been. Surprisingly, though, he responded as if she had spoken out loud. But then, to him, she probably had—he knew her so well now.

"I know you don't mean that as yes," he said

kindly. "In fact, I think you've already made up your mind about us." The statement gently prodded her to answer him truthfully, but the courage she needed would not come to her aid and she turned toward him in the night.

"No, darling, I haven't. Tonight just gave me a lot to think about, that's all." Her lips sought his, putting an end to any more questions. Aviva knew that she would continue to consider marrying Jeremy, but with each caress, each sweet kiss, her heart moved farther away from him. Self-preservation is a strong instinct, and while they made bittersweet love she had already begun to bury her heart so that she would no longer think about Jeremy Crowley when she could no longer have him.

Though she pretended to be asleep when Jeremy rose in the morning, Aviva watched his every move with hooded eyes. She wanted every inch of him imprinted in her memory forever. Watching him, she realized that all had not been lost.

The days and nights spent with him had been heavenly. Locked with Jeremy in their own world, Aviva had been happier than ever before. But in the year and a half since Sam's death she had done a lot of growing, maturing. Now she could think about the things that truly mattered in her life, make decisions that were weighed against all factors. Though she could not deny that walking away from Jeremy would be one of the hardest things she had ever done, she could also clearly see what she was walking toward.

When finally the door closed on Jeremy, she rose and showered, rubbing her cheek thoughtfully where

Jeremy had offered a lingering kiss, a kiss he hadn't known would be their last.

Slowly, reluctantly, she packed her bag, hoping against hope that Jeremy would call and offer some solution to her dilemma. But the phone was silent. Was he giving her room to breathe, to think?

By eleven Aviva had made arrangements to take the next flight back to Monterey. She didn't have to leave until noon to get to the airport on time, and for a while she sat staring at the piece of paper she had found in Jeremy's den. Then carefully, rationally, she began to write, explaining as best she could why she was leaving, going back to the inn. As she wrote Aviva found that, no matter how hard she tried, her feelings could never match the cold reality of her written words.

There was no way to rid herself of the memory of Jeremy. On command she could conjure up exactly how his skin felt as her fingertips ran over every inch of it, how his lips moved and molded under hers. Every now and again she stopped her writing, breathing deeply to control her shaking hand, tipping her head back to force the tears back into her eyes.

Suddenly the phone rang, its nerve-shattering jangle causing her to fairly jump from her seat. Instinctively, Aviva's hand reached out for the mechanism. Thinking better of it, she stopped her action, her hand hanging in midair as her mind considered what would happen if she were to answer the phone.

If the caller was Jeremy, one word from him could change her mind, make her stay, even though she knew it was not in her best interests. If it was Diane or one of the people from the party, the sound of her voice would be like pouring salt on an open wound.

Aviva drew her hand back, unwilling to take a chance either way. The phone rang and rang, and once again she found herself reaching out for it, now knowing that Jeremy was on the other end, willing to take care of her, wanting to love her. Just as she was about to give in, give up, the ringing stopped and she sank back into her chair feeling drained, uncertain.

Without a second thought she sprang from the chair and gathered her belongings. She set the note on the bedside table but could not resist one last loving feel of the bed where she had spent such happy moments. Then, with resolve pulled from the depths of her soul, she left the house, locking the door behind her—locking the door on the part of her dream that had to be put away.

Chapter Ten

"Thank you." Aviva paid the cabdriver and stood by her luggage as she watched the cab drive away. Turning back to the inn, she surveyed it for a moment and her heart jumped, warring with the excitement of being home and her sadness at being there alone. Sighing, she picked up her suitcase and walked up the brick path, pulled herself up the stairs and stood for a moment on the veranda; then, gathering her courage, she pushed open the door.

It was an eerie silence that swelled inside Whaler's Inn. No one came to greet her, no guests nodded as they walked past on their way out, and nothing had changed. Aviva could hear the crackle of the fire in the living room and the sound allowed her to relax a bit. Home. It was nice. The sounds, the rooms she loved. This was her place and it would ease her heavy heart in time. Turning toward the stairwell, Aviva decided to freshen up and compose herself before seeking out Jenny and Gladys. But she couldn't escape fast enough.

"Well, it looks like we've got a guest sneaking in

without registering." Gladys's voice cut into Aviva's mind, and as she turned, a smile plastered on her face, Jenny fell into her arms.

"Mommy, why didn't you call?" The little girl nuzzled her mother's neck and Aviva hugged her ever tighter, glad to be so loved.

"I'm sorry," Aviva said to Jenny, all the while looking at Gladys, a warning in her eyes, a warning that wasn't to be heeded.

"You're home far too early, Aviva," the old woman said, reprimand heavy in her voice, but Aviva would not be cowed.

"It's never too early to come home, Gladys. I think homesickness is the best excuse in the world to surprise everyone, don't you?" She tipped Jenny's face up and appeared engrossed in the little girl.

"I think so, too," Jenny agreed. "Did you bring Jeremy with you?"

Aviva's heart lurched. Thinking about him was hard enough, but hearing Jenny speak his name was devastating. "N-no—" she stumbled over the words "—he had to work. But we had a nice visit."

"Is that all?" Gladys broke in.

"Yes, that's all. It was a lovely visit and I'm glad to be home," Aviva reiterated.

"You certainly have a way with words, young woman. They say much more than one would think on the surface...."

"Gladys." This time Aviva commanded the woman's silence. This was her home, after all, her haven, and she would not be cross-examined by her boarder no matter how dear Gladys had become.

"All right. Just seems a mite funny to me." Gladys turned on her heel and headed toward the kitchen, mumbling that dinner would be early.

"Did you miss me, sweetheart?" Aviva asked Jenny once they were alone.

"Of course. But Gladys and Tim played with me. Cherry missed you."

"Did he really?" Aviva raised her eyebrows in surprise, a gesture that amused Jenny greatly.

"Do you want me to go get him?" Jenny offered, thoroughly excited by the prospect of the reunion.

"No," Aviva said slowly, "I think I'll clean up first and unpack, then I'll see Cherry." There would be no getting around the memories of Jeremy, Aviva realized as they talked about the dog. He had left his mark everywhere and she would simply have to live with it.

"Okay." Jenny hopped down from her mother's lap. "Shall I help you unpack?"

"I think I can handle it on my own," Aviva answered knowingly, "but I'll bet by the time dinner is on the table I'll have found a surprise in my suitcase for you."

"Oh, good." Jenny clapped her hands, having received the answer she expected, and ran off toward the kitchen. Heavily Aviva rose from the stair on which she sat and went to her room.

By the time Gladys announced dinner she had unpacked her case and washed her face. As they ate, Aviva filled in the curious old woman and little girl on a few of the details about her trip, careful to omit direct references to Jeremy. But Jenny wouldn't let her rest.

"But what about Jeremy?" she persisted. "Did he live in a nice house like us?"

"Yes, it was a nice house. A small house. Not half as nice as ours. I think you'd like the inn much better," Aviva explained patiently.

"Did he have a dog like Cherry?" The questions were going to be endless, it seemed, so as Aviva answered she also pulled out the package she had brought from Los Angeles.

"No, he doesn't have a dog like Cherry. But we got you a present." Aviva handed the bag to Jenny, who ripped it open and squealed with delight when she saw the bear.

"Can I call Jeremy and thank him?" Jenny asked immediately.

"No, I think he won't be home for a while. He's—" she was lying, something she had never done before "—working on a very important project. He'll call when he gets done with it." Aviva felt rather than saw Gladys's look of disapproval and straightened her shoulders against it. "Now, excuse yourself from the table and go get ready for bed."

"All right. 'Scuse me." Jenny climbed down from her chair, pecked Gladys's cheek, then kissed her mother's.

"I'll be up in a minute, honey." Aviva patted the little girl and turned her attention to her dessert when silence again descended on the room.

"You're not going to be able to live with it, Aviva," Gladys said from her end of the table.

"With what?" Aviva carefully raised her eyes to the old woman, keeping them cold and noncommittal.

"With what you feel for that man. I suggest that you think real hard before you throw him away."

"I didn't throw him away. It simply didn't work out, and I suggest that we consider Jeremy Crowley a closed subject."

Gladys nodded—a gesture that said so much—and unable to sit under her implied judgment any longer that night, Aviva pushed back her chair and left the room. She knew, of course, that Gladys was right. Obviously the homecoming was not going to be the emotional balm she expected, not with Gladys's all-seeing, all-knowing ways.

DAYS WORE ON at Whaler's Inn, and Aviva attacked the duties of the hotel with a vengeance, giving no one the opportunity to discuss Jeremy Crowley or her trip to Los Angeles. But despite her self-imposed activity Aviva began to succumb to the self-pity she had tried so hard to avoid.

The sound of the phone ringing sent jolts of anticipation through her and that day, four days after her return, Aviva couldn't resist answering it, knowing full well that Sue and Gladys would more than likely get it. After all, Jeremy's silence was not something she had anticipated. It was, if possible, even worse than if he had spent every waking moment writing her, calling her. She hadn't expected him simply to accept her disappearance without a fight, without some effort to bring her back. And deep in her heart she wished he would entice her back.

Gently, she lifted the receiver, half hoping, half

dreading that the voice on the other end would be Jeremy's.

"Yes, we have a beautiful room that looks out to the sea." Sue was talking to a prospective customer.

"Could we put in our reservations for a week from Tuesday?" the caller responded. "We'll stay three days."

"Certainly, sir," Sue answered. "We would appreciate it if you would send a fifty-dollar deposit for the room; our rates are..." Aviva gently lowered the receiver, knowing she had no reason to listen further, her hopes once again dashed.

Crossing to the window of her room, she looked out. She could see the windswept beach, the crashing waves of the ocean, but they brought her little relief from her sadness. The fog had rolled in, blanketing the land and casting an eerie glow about the inn. Aviva chuckled without mirth, wondering if that was what purgatory looked like: nothing defined, only the shadows of beauty, all surrounding the condemned soul, yet too far away to reach out and touch that which was wanted and needed so badly.

Quickly now Aviva allowed the feelings that had been hovering over her for so long to come to the surface. Perhaps if she grieved it would make the pain pass that much more quickly. She felt the need to relive the time she had spent with Jeremy Crowley. All along she had known it might not work, and she had accepted the fact that their relationship was not meant to be, but that didn't mean she couldn't miss him, long for him. Suddenly Aviva pulled herself back from the daydreams that threatened to consume her and stared at the door to her room. A knock, which she would have preferred not to answer, had sounded. But business and life went on.

"Come in," she called, moving away from the moody scene outside the window.

"Aviva." Gladys's tiny figure skittered into the room and she closed the door with a resounding thud. Aviva smiled as she always did now when she saw the woman's determined face. "I want this to stop right this minute."

"What are you talking about? Is someone giving you trouble?" Aviva answered, wondering what was amiss at the inn.

"You might call it trouble," Gladys said, settling herself on a chair.

"Okay, shoot. Who is it and I'll take care of it."

"It's you, young woman. I know you think you've done a dandy job of hiding your feelings from everyone around here but that's poppycock. You're either moving like a dervish through the inn or sitting around moping. Nobody knows what to do about you. You haven't got the time of day for your friends or your daughter. And you know that it's all true."

"Not really," Aviva answered, turning toward the mirror of her dressing table and picking up a brush.

"Don't act snooty with me, Miss. You know good and well that Jeremy is preying on your mind night and day. I've given you four days and I think it's time you give up or do something about your situation."

Aviva sighed, put down her brush and turned to Gladys. "All right. I agree I haven't been myself. But

I certainly wouldn't characterize my behavior as erratic. Nor would I say I am neglecting my daughter. Now, you're just going to have to realize that some people need a little space when they hurt. After all, you've been doing it for years and I doubt that anyone ever tried to tell you to snap out of it," Aviva lectured Gladys, but the harsh words were softened by a smile of sweet sadness on her face. "Listen, Gladys, I appreciate what you're trying to do. Really. But just let me have my moment. I promise you, in another few days I'll be my old self. And if it will make you feel any better, I promise to spend more time with Jenny. But, please, give me time."

"Aviva—" Gladys's tone was gentle now "—you may not get another chance."

"I know that."

"Then are you sure leaving Jeremy was the right thing? I mean, wasn't there some way to work out your differences?" Gladys probed on, but Aviva couldn't be angry. She was sure Gladys was simply reliving her own life and didn't want Aviva to make the same mistakes.

"I'm not altogether sure. I do believe that my coming back here alone was best for me in some ways. It made me realize my obligations were so great that I couldn't take the chance of ruining the life I had built. And I suppose it's obvious by my behavior that I miss him dreadfully." She offered a half smile. "But he probably realizes that it was the best thing, too. I haven't heard from him since I've been back. Not a letter, not a phone call. We're both adults. Jeremy and I knew when it was time to let go."

"Well, I think you're both crazy," Gladys mumbled.

"Gladys, I'm too tired to argue. My heart just isn't in it. So if that's what you believe, then we'll just have to leave it at that, won't we?" Aviva sat calmly, waiting for the old woman to speak. She knew there was no way to stop a conversation with her other than to refuse to go on with it. Yet her words reverberated in Aviva's mind. She might never have another chance.

"All right, all right," Gladys said, rising and walking to the door. "But just know that men like Jeremy Crowley don't come waltzing into your house every day of the week. Call him. Try to work this out."

"Don't you think I haven't thought of it? Don't you believe that I think about him every waking moment?" Aviva protested. "But it's a two-way street, you know."

"Maybe," Gladys answered, "but that's an awfully old-fashioned way of looking at things, if you ask me. You just think about it. Think about how life will be when you're my age, then tell me that you're going to wait for him to make the first move."

"I was simply being rhetorical. As far as I'm concerned it was wonderful while it lasted. But it's over and done with and that's final." Aviva raised an eyebrow, daring Gladys to try to continue the conversation. But the older woman saw her determination, sighed and left the room without another word.

For a moment Aviva sat in the silence of her room considering the advice. Gladys knew how deep her emotions ran—deep and confused. Yet the one shining truth was that the inn and Jenny were still hers, and that thought must remain with her always. Rising from her dressing chair, Aviva followed Gladys out the door and stood for a minute on the landing.

Pride welled inside her as she looked about at what she had created. It was good to be needed at the inn—her inn—and standing there she knew she could exist without Jeremy in her world. But she couldn't deny the sparkle he had brought to her life. A sad smile parted her lips and Aviva moved, taking that first step that would lead her down into the very core of the life she was protecting.

THE EVENING PROGRESSED PLEASANTLY. Aviva enjoyed the conversation and the fact that almost everyone had turned in early after coffee. Only the Andersons had gone out for dinner that night. Jenny was in bed by ten and Aviva had the house to herself.

As she roamed about the gigantic inn she tried to recapture the feeling she had had standing alone on the landing. Where was the pride in accomplishment now? In the darkened halls there now seemed to be only loneliness. Finally, settling herself in the living room, Aviva picked up a book that lay on the window seat. Settling herself back, she opened it.

It was one of Jeremy's, a thin volume of poetry. Amazing that no one had put it on the bookshelf. Perhaps it was fate, her final exorcism. Clutching it to her breast, Aviva slipped her legs underneath her and waited, wondering if somehow she could gain some deeper understanding of her warring feelings by clutching that small possession close to her.

Opening it, she curled herself into a ball and began

to read, her eyes only scanning the pages. Oh, the memories the little book held.

The sound of wheels on gravel almost escaped her notice as she sat lost in dreams. But rousing herself for an instant, Aviva peeked out of the lace-covered window. She could not make out the car, given the darkness of the night and the swirl of the fog, but from the shape of it she knew it was the Andersons returning. Settling back down, she thought how wrong one could be about people.

That young couple had struck her as partying people. Well, maybe they found Carmel too tame for their taste. Turning her attention back to the book, she prayed that they would simply go to their room. She didn't want visitors that night. Not when she was finally making friends again with herself...and with the memory of Jeremy.

Quietly she waited, listening for the door to open and close. But instead, the bell sounded. She must have locked it out of force of habit. Well, now if they wanted to chat, it was her own fault.

Flipping her hair behind her shoulders, Aviva went to the door and reached for the knob. Her heart stopped for an instant. It wasn't locked. Tentatively she turned the brass knob and then opened the door a crack to peek out. Aviva blinked. The fog was playing tricks on her. Slowly she stepped back, opening the door ever wider.

"Got a room, lady? I've been traveling a long way." Jeremy's soft voice floated over her, and Aviva simply stared at what must surely be an apparition. Her heart ceased to beat, her breath stopped for a mo-

ment. Then she was engulfed in the strong arms of
Jeremy Crowley, and his silly green plaid hat fell to
the floor as he twirled her about him. No ghost could
hold her as dearly as he did then, and Aviva closed her
eyes against the happiness, knowing that her mind
might have decided that she could do without him,
but surely her heart never could.

"How—how—" She could not speak, her joy was
too great. What did it matter how he happened to be
there? All that mattered was that she was in his arms
once more, safe because they were standing in the
inn—together.

"I drove off course." His soft voice teased her, and
Aviva's arms tightened in response. How could he
joke at a time like this, she wondered, her question
negated by her sheer, unadulterated happiness at his
presence.

"Did you really think I would let you go so easily,
you silly woman?" he demanded, holding her at arm's
length. "How could you do such a thing? Running
away, not even trusting me enough to help work things
out. Aviva, I ought to wring your pretty little neck."

"Oh, Jeremy, it just seemed so hopeless. I knew
you couldn't live without certain things, and I just
couldn't live with them. You have to respect that,"
she said, suddenly sobered, wondering if he was going
to ask her to go back to L.A. with him.

"I do accept that. That's why I'm here." Her face
brightened, and he immediately held up a warning
hand. "I didn't say I'm here to do things your way,
although you could be quite persuasive if you had a
mind to."

"Then what? I'm not going back with you." Her face set in a determined grimace and Jeremy smiled at her, a gesture she could not resist although she tried to desperately.

"Stop it, Jeremy. I mean what I say," she reiterated, "but I am so glad to see you."

"That's more like it," he said, capturing her hands in his. "Now that I know you didn't leave for any other reason but your own snobbishness, I'll tell you what I propose to do with the rest of our lives."

Aviva went willingly when he led her to the bottom step and sat her down. Towering above her he clasped his hands behind his back, looking as stern as he possibly could.

"Now, I want you to know that I am not giving in to you," he began as she watched him pace back and forth. "I have my pride, too. However, I am also a practical man. I know that it is much easier to run my business from here than it is for you to move the inn to Los Angeles." He cocked an eyebrow at her and Aviva responded, careful not to jump to any conclusions.

"I'll agree to that, sir," Aviva said slowly, wondering where this was all leading.

"Therefore, I propose that we get married and live right here in Carmel with Gladys, Jenny, Cherry and anyone else you feel you need around you to make life worth living." Aviva smiled, loving his light-hearted manner, loving the fact that he still wanted her, understood how important her life in Carmel was. But her soaring heart was immediately captured and brought down to earth as he continued to speak.

"But I will not have a wife who shirks her duties—"

Immediately she stopped him. "I never had any intention of doing that and you know it!" she replied indignantly.

"I know, darling." Jeremy had sunk to the floor, kneeling at her feet and taking her hands in his. "I'm just kidding. But I'm not kidding when I say that you must understand that part of my life that you do not like."

Aviva lowered her eyes, knowing what was coming: He was going to insist that they spend part of their time in Los Angeles with those people. But what if he did? Couldn't she make such a small sacrifice for his obviously large one?

"I will have to continue to associate with the crowd we were with the other night. Again, I ask you simply to accept them for what they are. If I promise to take you to L.A. only when it's absolutely necessary, to deliver you always safely home to Whaler's Inn each time we leave, to care for you and love you and treasure you always, couldn't you be my Los Angeles wife every once in a while? Could you accept that much? Then, maybe, you'll see that I love you more than any place, any other people and any other thing in my life. Maybe then the love I have for you will show you that there is nothing in this entire world to be afraid of, to run from. Aviva, will you be my wife and accept what I have to give you?"

"Oh, God, Jeremy, yes, yes, yes." She was on her feet, her lips on his before his smile could completely burst forth. As his arms tightened about her and his tongue parted her lips, Aviva offered a prayer of thanks, crushing into him until she felt that they could be no closer. Unable to stop it, she felt a shiver run through her body, and she hugged him ever closer, her head now resting on his shoulder.

"I'd like to think I caused that reaction, love, but I think it's the chilly fog that's causing the shiver," Jeremy whispered into her hair.

"Don't believe it for an instant." Aviva sighed happily. "But I suppose we should close the door if we're going to be carrying on like this." Reluctantly, she rose and shut the door against the night that seemed less black and foreboding. Turning back, she looked at Jeremy. How beautiful he looked to her at that moment and how beautiful he would look, she knew, when he was gray with the years.

"What are you thinking?" he asked, his grin firmly in place.

"Just what a beautiful life we're going to have together. You and I..."

"And Jenny," he added before she could finish.

"And Jenny," Aviva said, moving toward him and winding her arms about his neck.

"Now that I'm going to have a daughter, what do you say we continue this upstairs behind closed doors? I'll have to get used to such things," Jeremy whispered, running his hands up the length of her spine, making Aviva melt into him.

"I'm glad to see you've considered everything carefully," Aviva whispered.

"I have, Aviva. You have to believe that." Jeremy's hands captured her face, forcing her to look into his eyes. There she could see the depth of love, the force of his commitment and the breadth of his sincerity, and finally Aviva Thompson felt safe.

"I believe you" was all she could say.

"Then let's go tuck our daughter in for the night." Gently Jeremy took her hands in his, rose to his feet, and kissed her lightly before leading her up the stairs—a walk to heaven for Aviva, for with each step the past fell away, leaving only the present and dreams of the future.

An epic novel of exotic rituals and the lure of the Upper Amazon

THE TAKERS
RIVER OF GOLD

JERRY AND S.A. AHERN

THE TAKERS are the intrepid Josh Culhane and the seductive Mary Mulrooney. These two adventurers launch an incredible journey into the Brazilian rain forest. Far upriver, the jungle yields its deepest secret—the lost city of the Amazon warrior women!

THE TAKERS series is making publishing history. Awarded *The Romantic Times* first prize for High Adventure in 1984, the opening book in the series was hailed by *The Romantic Times* as "the next trend in romance writing and reading. Highly recommended!"

Jerry and S.A. Ahern have never been better!

TAK–3

You're invited to accept 4 books and a surprise gift Free!

Acceptance Card

Mail to: **Harlequin Reader Service®**

In the U.S.
2504 West Southern Ave.
Tempe, AZ 85282

In Canada
P.O. Box 2800, Postal Station A
5170 Yonge Street
Willowdale, Ontario M2N 6J3

YES! Please send me 4 free Harlequin American Romance® novels and my free surprise gift. Then send me 4 brand new novels as they come off the presses. Bill me at the low price of $2.25 each —an 11% saving off the retail price. There are no shipping, handling or other hidden costs. There is no minimum number of books I must purchase. I can always return a shipment and cancel at any time. Even if I never buy another book from Harlequin, the 4 free novels and the surprise gift are mine to keep forever.

154 BPA-BPGE

Name	(PLEASE PRINT)	
Address		Apt. No.
City	State/Prov.	Zip/Postal Code

This offer is limited to one order per household and not valid to present subscribers. Price is subject to change.

ACAR-SUB-1

Readers rave about
Harlequin American Romance!

" ...the best series of modern romances
I have read...great, exciting, stupendous,
wonderful."

 —S.E., *Coweta, Oklahoma*

" ...they are absolutely fantastic...going to be
a smash hit and hard to keep on the
bookshelves."

 —P.D., Easton, Pennsylvania

"The American line is great. I've enjoyed
every one I've read so far."

 —W.M.K., Lansing, Illinois

" ...the best stories I have read in a long
time."

 —R.H., Northport, New York

Names available on request.